About the autho

D. M. Jones was born in Bradford to immigrant parents from the former Yugoslavia. She was raised in Denholme (West Yorkshire), a small village where her parents worked in Fosters Mill. Dani wrote her first play at primary school and went on to Keighley Girls' Grammar School, where she spent most of her time singing, dancing and getting into trouble.

At the age of seventeen she joined the civil service and stayed until 1975 when she left to have her first baby, with another following a year later. When she was forty, she returned to education and gained a BA (Hons) in home and community studies. After gaining a PGCE in further education, she went on to study counselling and psychotherapy. She had a variety of jobs which all involved people, in the social sector and in the private sector, along with running a successful private practice in counselling.

The one thing about Dani is that once you have met her you will never forget her. Her positive attitude, storytelling and ability to make you laugh make her a natural comedienne whose observations on life cannot fail to amuse.

by the same author
Chasing Rainbows
(The first in a trilogy)

Vanguard Press, 2020

OCEANS AWAY

D.M. Jones

OCEANS AWAY

Vanguard Press

VANGUARD PAPERBACK

© Copyright 2021
D.M. Jones

The right of D.M. Jones to be identified as author of
this work has been asserted by her in accordance with the
Copyright, Designs and Patents Act 1988.

A CIP catalogue record for this title is
available from the British Library.

ISBN 978-1-80016-159-7

Vanguard Press is an imprint of
Pegasus Elliot MacKenzie Publishers Ltd.
www.pegasuspublishers.com.

First Published in 2021

Vanguard Press
Sheraton House Castle Park
Cambridge England

Printed & Bound in Great Britain

Dedication

I dedicate this book to the people who have supported me on my journey. You have made me laugh and some of you have made me cry. Without you I would not be who I am today, and you all sail with me on life's ocean.

Without the craziness of my life and the people who have touched my heart I would never have known love and warmth of feeling. The tears, the hurt and the disappointments were worth all the memories.

'Tomorrow is as invisible as the moon on a sunny day.'

Acknowledgements

I was not expecting to publish this book so quickly. It had to be, as readers are very demanding. So, I wish to thank them all for their support and inspiring comments.

Caroline Anne Fawcett, you have been my partner in crime, always! We hold each other's hands and you dry my tears. You are part of the great adventure that enables my stories. You are an awesome woman who laughs with me and straightens my crown. Like Siamese twins our lives are entwined.

Debra Helen Winton, you always have an opinion that is listened to (not always acted upon) and you are always there. You are a major name on my list of what I am grateful for. The daughter I never had.

Phillip Goodhand Tait, you were surely sent by the universe to give me your songs to inspire my books. Your kindness is awesome and I shall always be indebted to you.

I have to mention John Jones who pushed me to submit this book and he gives me the time and space to be myself. Without his support I would not be able to bring my work to the people.

A new addition to my clan is Lucie Dowling. A beautiful actress whose help and advice have been invaluable. You remind me so much of myself at your age Lucie and we have become firm friends, sharing and caring. You inspire me to continue writing and I love you for it.

Carol Towers you say it like it is and I am indebted to you for your comments and editing. You are far away and yet so close!

I also wish to thank all those (there are too many of you to name individually) who have added to my experiences and my journey which has allowed my imagination to run wild across the pages.

OCEANS AWAY

Don't wake me up if I should be dreaming
I don't want to miss one minute of this dream.
Don't worry now, you're not dreaming.
I'll always love you wherever you'll be.
Oceans away go where you may
Love will be with you, oceans away.
Love will be with you, oceans away.
The night is cold, but day is certain
No twilight zone can last very long.
Darkness my friend I hide in your curtain
If you're not here with me, please let me dream on
Oceans away, go where you may.
Love will be with you, oceans away.
Love will be with you, oceans away.

Phillip Goodhand Tait

Chapter One

Stephen, the administrator of the Flight Aviation Authority, sent his chauffeur to meet Felix and take him to his hotel. Felix scanned the sea of boards, held by strangers all waiting for someone, until he found his name. He was glad to get off the plane and be away from Olivia and part of his past that he was not proud of. He made his way over to a small Italian looking man and announced that he was Felix Schwarz.

"I am Danny, please to come this way with me, the car is right outside." Danny took Felix's case and shuffled his way through the myriads of people who didn't seem to know where they were going. He stopped beside a massive, shiny cream Cadillac. Not the type of car that Felix was expecting at all. He was used to New York's yellow cabs.

As they walked through the exit Felix did a quick scan round to see if he could see Olivia, but there were so many people it would have been impossible. Well, it didn't matter as his arrogance assured him that she would ring him when she had the time. How could she resist him?

Stephen Baxter and Felix were due to meet later in the week to finalise months of negotiations that would culminate in Felix's employers beginning internal flights in some states across America. Danny never stopped talking and his words became a drone as Felix tuned out and into his thoughts about the flight. He relived his apology to Olivia and thought he couldn't have done better and that fate had brought them together once more as they flew over the Atlantic

Felix was a true Capricorn. He was an ambitious man with an overly optimistic attitude bordering on arrogance. That arrogance could sometimes get the better of him. This time, though, he had excelled in humility as he grovelled to Olivia in the hope that he might see her whilst in New York. He had one motive and one motive only; that was to once more savour the pleasures of the wild woman he'd bedded in Hamburg all those years ago. He had never forgotten that night, nor that body.

What Felix didn't realise was that his words had been dancing in the dark and Olivia had absolutely no intention of ever thinking about Felix again, let alone sleeping with him. He was gone with each tear that rolled down her cheeks after he returned to his seat on the plane to sit next to his new friend, Adam. Both men were totally deluded if they thought they might be seeing Olivia again. They were in a past that was gone; way back over twenty years before.

Danny's voice brought Felix back from his daydream. "Sorry Sir, there seems to be a hold-up in front, we might be here a while. There are drinks in the back if you care for one." Felix found the drinks and was amazed at the array of spirits before him. It wasn't long before he was sipping a brandy, allowing the warm glow of the nectar to enter his nether regions. He lay back on the plush navy blue, suede seat and closed his eyes. It wasn't long before he was back in Hamburg with the woman who categorically stated that they would not be having sex that night, just because a clairvoyant, weeks before, predicted it would happen.

Just as he was giving up on his quest, the little minx with the big brown eyes, threw her nightdress across the room and pounced on him. The events that followed made it a night to remember. As he took another sip of the brandy there was a slight twitch down below. He looked down and saw that his nether regions were beginning to quiver. That part of him he thought of as redundant was now coming alive. He downed the remnants of his glass and poured himself another drink. His thoughts returned to Hamburg, and he began to savour the memory of a love juice he'd never tasted before or since that amazing night.

The limousine slowly made its way towards Queensboro Bridge. Then without warning the traffic stopped. After speaking to the traffic policeman who was going down the line explaining to drivers what had happened, Danny turned to speak to Felix. "There was an accident and we could be here for a while. I can turn round and we can take a different route through Queens but it might take longer?" Felix decided it would be best to not stay in the queue as he might just finish the bottle of brandy off, and he was eager to get to the Hotel. Once he got started on brandy, he found it hard to say no.

It wasn't that long before they were zooming through Queens towards the city. "Danny, could you put the screen up please I might just have a cat nap?" As the dark screen rose the back windows began to darken also. There was much privacy to be had! This was good as the thunderbolt in his trousers was throbbing and needed attention. His thoughts of Olivia kept the momentum of his earlier stirrings.

Felix let out a sigh of relief as his 'dorje' exploded neatly into his handkerchief. He liked the word dorje, it sounded so much more romantic than 'penis'. Dorje, is a Tibetan word representing indestructibility, firmness of spirit and spiritual power. This was apt as Felix definitely felt a firmness and much spiritual power after all that brandy. There was always a firmness ready in Felix and his quests for sexual pleasure could be insatiably indestructible. He was constantly in pursuit of the yoni. He had mastered the art of seduction and yet all that was thrown out of the window one night in Hamburg when the crazy woman from Yorkshire took over. The art of seduction means nothing when lust becomes the name of the game.

It wasn't long before the cream Cadillac pulled up outside the Moxy, a hotel which was in a perfect location to access all that New York had to offer. Felix stayed at the Moxy on many occasions as it was only five minutes away from his favourite place; Times Square. He didn't plan on spending much time in the hotel and was booked into a queen room which was clean, plain and functional. All he needed now was to catch up on some sleep.

After unpacking and showering, he picked up an envelope that Danny gave to him before he drove away. Inside was a short, handwritten note.

You are cordially invited to join me and my friends for a dinner at mine on this coming Thursday at seven.

It was a good job that Felix packed his tuxedo. He was prepared for every occasion but thought he might just go out and buy a new shirt for this important dinner date as he needed to create an impression.

After a long nap Felix woke to see that night had arrived and he was very hungry. After a meal of scallops and zucchini he made his way to the roof-top bar with the intention of having just a few drinks and then an early night. The bar was empty apart from two old women who looked like sisters huddled together in a corner, laughing. He nodded politely at them before sitting by the end of the veranda where he could look out over the city. A city that looked like an amazing firework frozen in time. A solo sax player sat in the corner, a sad blues tune permeated the air creating a calm, relaxing atmosphere.

Felix didn't notice the man who sat a few tables away from him until he heard his voice. An English accent stands out when abroad, a Yorkshire voice stands out even more. Felix saw Adam speaking to the waiter. "So, what is that one then, mate?" Adam was pointing at the drinks' menu and the waiter was explaining the list of ingredients in the cocktails that were taking Adam's fancy. After making his choice Adam coughed and looked around the roof top. His eyes met Felix's and they both laughed. He nodded in acknowledgement and mouthed as his index finger pointed downwards, "You staying here?" Felix nodded.

It wasn't long before they were chatting together as though they had been friends for years. "So, what do you think Adam, are you up for it?" Felix asked as he summoned the waiter to bring more drinks. Both men were slurring their words as their alcohol consumption got the better of them and they were still tired from the long flight from Manchester.

Adam slurred back, "well you only live once, so I will put myself in your capable hands Felix. Let's do it."

Felix suggested that the following evening they should visit Flushings, China Town, for a massage. They both had heavy schedules the next day and a relaxing massage would be just the tonic they needed. Felix had been to China Town for a massage many times and he omitted to say that the girls on Fortieth Road were rather accomplished at massaging a man's middle leg with both hands and mouth. He thought it would be a big welcome surprise for Adam.

Adam really liked Felix, despite what he'd done to Olivia. He never told Felix about his affair with her. Whereas Felix had one night of lust with her before Adam met her and Adam had more than a year of love with her. Felix didn't need to know that. Adam was looking forward to some adventures and Felix was just the man to take him on them, as he seemed to know his way around and Adam wondered what else they might do while he was in the city. Just before he fell asleep that night Adam's thoughts wandered to Olivia and he wondered if she might ring him before too long. He felt that the bond between them had never really been broken and now he had seen her after so many years had passed, he was beginning to review his feelings. He didn't feel good about his past behaviours and thought that he could make up for them. He hoped she would call.

He looked at his watch. It would be nine a.m. in Bradford. He picked up his phone and dialled his secretary's number. "Hi, Jean, it's me. I have a job for you." Jean took up her pen. "I need you to find somebody for me. I have no idea where she is staying but she came in on the flight from Manchester. This is a long shot and if you can't find her don't worry about it. Her name is Olivia Orphanidis. When you find her send her some sunflowers and lilacs!" Jean said that she would be right on it. "Thanks love and no, there is no message." Adam fell asleep and dreamt of afternoons of love on the river Ouse, near York, holding the woman with the big brown eyes.

The next night Adam and Felix were on their way to 'Nai Nai Shu Fang's Amno Shi'. "So, do you know this woman, Felix?" Adam was curious about the woman who owned the place. "Shu Fang means kind. Didn't you say it was Chinese?" Felix was impressed. "How do you know that?" Adam replied, "I don't know."

"Yes, she is very Chinese; been here for years. She was one of the masseurs once upon a time, a very long time ago. Rumour has it that she won the place in a card game and now she owns it. Her granddaughters, Ling and Lang do most of the work. They are very accomplished and I never miss a session with them when I am over here."

Adam thought for a moment and asked, "What do you mean with them?"

"Oh, nothing, that was a slip of the tongue." Having just got to know Adam he was not prepared to share all of what he did with him. He was soon beginning to realise that this Yorkshire man was a bit wet behind the ears and more than a tad naïve.

It wasn't long before they were sitting in a large room that was covered in gold flock wallpaper with red organza curtains hanging at intervals round the walls. There was also red organza hanging from the roof which divided the room into sections. Two large massage beds crowded each corner and a massive round bed sat in the centre of the room. It was strewn with black satin cushions. Adam nearly jumped out of his skin when music began to play. Keith Sweat began to sing 'Nobody' just as two slight girls came into the room. The girls were dressed in long silk black kaftans. They were sheer and left nothing to the imagination. Soon Adam and Felix were in different corners with their clothes neatly folded on golden chairs, that weren't for sitting on. As Ling poured cedarwood and bergamot oils on Adam's back, he jumped. "You OK, sir, it not too hot, for you?"

"No, it's fine, sorry love I was drifting off." Ling began to spread the oil gently across Adam's back and he was soon floating in dreamland as the essence of herbs, began to permeate his brain and the soft hands began to work their magic. He'd never had a massage like this and when Ling's hand met the back of his love sacs, she slowly stroked them. He became aroused as he felt a stirring in his loins. He was glad that he was lying on his stomach as something was happening that he couldn't control.

"May you be so kind as to turn over now, Mr?" Adam turned on the bed and his manhood sprung forth in a massive greeting. Ling took a

18

towel and covered it so that Adam would be saved from the embarrassment of not being able to control himself. She continued the massage and discreetly left Adams nether bits out of her routine. When she finished the magic with her hands and Adam was more relaxed than he had ever been in his life, Ling produced a rainbow-coloured glass butt plug. Adam was up for new experiences, but he knew where to draw the line.

"Ling, no, I am sorry, but I am not like that." The butt plug disappeared as quickly as it arrived.

"OK, so you like *afellio*?" Well, Adam had no idea what that was and he just couldn't say no, twice. He was too polite for that. Ling produced a blindfold. "You put this on, is best when not seeing. It heightens the senses. Do not be afraid this is good. You trust me?" Adam nodded.

Suddenly the music changed from sexy sultry to Tomaso Albinoni's *Adagio in G minor*. Adam remembered the music from the horse scene in the film, *The Godfather*. He soon forgot all about the horse as he felt two small hands dancing to the music on his middle leg, which he felt would surely burst. Wow, this was something else and then it became something else, as he lost himself in the music and the pleasurable feeling of the mouth that was now sucking and sometimes nibbling at his shaft. Ling was certainly right about the blindfold heightening his senses. This was pure heaven. It wasn't long before Adam could hold back no longer and the gates of his passion blew off as the recipient of the contents swallowed hard. He thought he was about to disappear into the mouth that had enchanted his manhood. This was a gobbler unleashed.

As the music came to a close, Adam felt that he was alone. He removed the blindfold from his eyes and looked across at Felix who was now on the bed in the middle of the room, with Lang. He was taken aback as Ling joined them and he could not keep his eyes away from the trio now writhing and squirming beyond the see-through curtain. Arms and legs entwined like three serpents in a dance of sensuality. Adam wondered whether perhaps he might try a threesome, one day, as he fell asleep; only to be woken by Ling who asked him, "You have tea now?"

Adam nodded and Ling returned with some butterfly tea. Adam was a true Yorkshire man and didn't really like trying new things. The blue tea had flower petals in it and didn't taste that bad. Ling explained the properties of the tea. "You wanna buy some, I sell you." Adam nodded. He could give it to his secretary, Jean, as a gift.

Ling rang a bell and a very old looking lady came across the room holding a small blue carrier bag. She bowed to Adam and handed him the tea. As she did so she smiled a toothless smile and winked at him. His eyes followed her as she shuffled across the room, and he was more than taken aback when the old lady turned and gave him the OK sign.

It wasn't until later, back at the hotel that Adam thought he might have a heart attack. He and Felix were discussing the night over a couple of brandies. "Yes, Adam, I always have them both. I love threesomes especially with two women." Felix went on. "I should get the video in a few days." Adam took a sip of his drink and then another sip.

"What video?"

Felix began to laugh. "Don't worry Adam you weren't filmed. I had to pay extra but it will be worth it." Adam always thought he was rather cosmopolitan and a man of the world, even though he had never eaten rice till he was forty. He now realised that perhaps he wasn't.

"Well, Felix, I am really up for new experiences but when Ling produced that glass thing! I drew the line at anybody putting something up my arse." They both laughed and Felix called the waiter and ordered more drinks.

They sat in a comfortable silence for a few minutes with their own thoughts, before Adam asked, "Did you see the old woman, the old woman who brought me tea? She was really old."

"You mean Shu Fang? Yes, I told you about her. She owns the place." Felix took a drink. "Why do you ask me?"

Adam was puzzled and continued, "Well when she brought the tea, she winked at me."

"Did she now? Did she give you an OK sign too?" Adam nodded. Felix went on as he thought he had best enlighten Adam. "You got top marks then."

"Felix, what do you mean, top marks for what?"

Felix thought that surely Adam couldn't be so naïve? "Adam, were you blindfolded?"

Adam nodded once more. "Ling said it would enhance the pleasure and I needed to trust."

"And did it?" Felix asked.

"Did it? Goodness, it was amazing. I have never felt anything like it before. In fact, I might go back, before I leave, for another session."

Felix leaned towards Adam as he said, "Then that is all you need to know." Then he winked and gave the OK sign. Adam wasn't best pleased as he felt that Felix knew more than he was letting on.

"No, it's not, I need you to explain." Felix winked and gave the OK sign to Adam again. The mist began to lift and Adam sat back. "You mean?"

"Yes, it wasn't Ling giving you the *afellio*, it was the grandmother. Do you want another drink?" Adam was so shocked by what he'd just been told. "I'll get these Felix. I think I need a double, maybe a triple."

After a few more drinks Felix's tongue loosened, and he began to talk about his experience in Hamburg with Olivia. The way he recounted the event showed him to be rather chauvinistic with an arrogant attitude towards women. Adam didn't like what he was hearing but continued to smile and nod in the appropriate places. He could see that they were different when it came to the fairer sex. Adam was always looking for the love in his life whereas Felix was always looking for the next quick fix to ease his aching scrotum.

Later, when alone in his room Adam went over all that Felix said. His attitude did not stop him liking the man, as he knew people were all different and he was quite accepting of what Felix thought although he hadn't liked having to listen about the encounter in Hamburg.

The next morning Adam saw Felix in reception as he was leaving the building and decided he needed to speak to him. As he put his hand on Felix's shoulder he said, "Great night, last night, mate. Have you time for a quick word." Felix looked at his watch and nodded.

Adam wasn't sure what he was going to say but knew that he had to say something. "Thanks for sharing last night. You certainly have been around the houses, haven't you? You know we are similar in many ways. You could be my brother form another mother. I just felt that I needed to give you some advice." Felix wondered what on earth could Adam be wanting to give him advice about. He nodded once more, "Sure you can." He'd already decided he wouldn't be taking advice from a man who came from Yorkshire and wasn't as worldly as he made out.

Adam began, "In my experience I have found that sometimes my past has caught up with me and bit me on the backside. I wouldn't like to be in your shoes if some of those women you talked about last night ever caught up with you!" What Adam hadn't realized was that he'd met someone more arrogant than he was and Felix didn't seem very happy about Adam's advice. Felix shrugged Adam's comment off with a blunt retort that left Adam speechless. He walked away quickly and was greeted by Danny at the door. He did not look back. Adam stood in the middle of reception. 'Well, mate, thanks a lot!' he thought. 'There was no need for that. I hope one day that you get your comeuppance and not before too long?' Little did Adam know that his wish was soon to be realised and Felix was just about to get the shock of his life.

CHAPTER TWO

It wasn't long before Thursday came around and once more Felix was sitting in the back of the cream Cadillac with the blue seats. Danny, the driver, didn't stop talking for the first ten miles until Felix asked if he could play some music. He didn't really want to listen to the Bronx twang any more and was feeling a little nervous and rather dubious about the evening ahead. The whole of Felix's future was resting on his meeting with Stephen Baxter. The legal teams had done their work and it was all about the handshake now.

"Have you a preference, sir?"

Felix thought for a moment. "Yes, Danny, can you find me some Hauser. It wasn't long before Felix was relaxing to Hauser and Senorita, singing 'I Will Always Love You'. Not many people can sing Whitney Houston songs, but this lady certainly could, and the tones of Hauser's cello made it a masterpiece. He was lost in the music when Danny turned into Alpine, in New Jersey. Alpine was only fifteen miles from the centre of Manhattan and housed some of the richest people in the region. This was obvious by the magnificent mansions that they were now passing and the delicately cut grass verges that graced the sidewalks.

Danny turned right towards some beautiful large filigree gates which opened like magic. As they drove up the long drive bordered by purple hydrangeas, Felix saw a sight to behold. Before him, there was a French chateau painted in lilac. It was very impressive and it was hard to believe that he was not in the Dordogne. A splendid courtyard of grey slate cobbles, expertly placed to make a pattern of what seemed like trees, spread out before a magnificent double stained, glass door which opened immediately as the car stopped. A small pretty woman ran down the steps. She was wearing a blue dress and a cream apron. She curtsied to

Felix before throwing her arms round Danny. "I missed you this morning my love."

Danny looked rather embarrassed and quickly looked around to make sure there was no one about. He took hold of Diana's arms and gently pushed her away. "You know you mustn't do this. It is not right; not right in front of the house." Diana bowed her head before addressing Felix.

"I am so sorry, sir, but I not see my husband this morning and I love him much." So, this was Danny's wife!

Felix asked Danny how long they had been married. "Many, many years, sir." Felix couldn't believe it as Diana didn't look old enough.

"Well congratulations, may you have many, many more." Diana picked up Felix's bag.

"Please come with me." On the way to the room where Felix would spend the night, Diana never stopped talking; just like her husband. "We are on Rio Vista, and it is a very special place. Danny and I are very lucky to work here. The madam treats me very nice."

Before Diana left Felix, she told him that the Baxter's were out but would be back for the dinner party later. He walked to the large window that overlooked a lake and was overwhelmed by the opulence of his surroundings. Although it was a warm sunny day, a small fire burned under an ornate mantelpiece that should have graced an apartment in Rome. A large bed covered in cream and midnight blue silk cushions crowded the room. He lay down on the bed to look up at a large, panelled ceiling that met in a point and from which hung the most magnificent multi-coloured, crystal chandelier. Felix had only ever seen clear crystal chandeliers. This one could have been the ninth wonder in the world. As the sun began to drop down towards the horizon, the chandelier caught the rays and sent a display of rainbow colours around the room.

Felix looked at his watch and decided to take a walk to the lake before his bath. He passed a pool, a summer house and three guest houses on his tour of the gardens. There was serious money here. As the sun disappeared beyond the horizon Felix made his way to the kitchen where Diana was busy putting finishing touches to the dishes which were to be served later. She didn't see him and quickly went through to the dining room where she began to lay the table. Felix entered behind and watched her for a while, wondering if perhaps he should make a move on her. He had no scruples.

This room could have graced the Louvre and took one back in time, to the days of Marie Antoinette. Antique crockery with pink roses on a pale blue background and edged in gold was systematically laid around a highly polished mahogany table. Crystal wine glasses of blue and gold, which could have been Bohemian, lined up on the table like soldiers on parade. Felix recognised the gold Caccia cutlery which must have cost thousands.

He coughed and Diana turned quickly. "Can I help you, sir?" she asked.

"Yes please, Diana, could I perhaps get a drink?" Calling people by their first name makes them feel special, or so Felix thought.

"Come with me, sir." Diana took him back to his room.

Once inside she shut the door and Felix thought, 'Hello, is it playtime?' Diana walked over to a copy of Monet's *Water Lilies*. It was hard to tell that it was a copy. Diana pressed one of the lilies and the picture slid up the damask wallpaper and an amazing shelf covered in drinks to suit every palate slowly made its way out of the hole in the wall. He was overawed and didn't notice Diana curtsey as she left the room. As he was deciding which drink to have first there was a tiny rap at the door and Diana re-entered the room.

"Sorry sir I forgot to say that before dinner, drinks will be served in the orangery at six thirty."

"Thank you, Diana." Felix returned to his task and wondered where the orangery might be. He was sure that he would find it. He took a short nap and then began to prepare for the evening. He couldn't escape the way his body looked, whilst showering, as the whole bathroom was hi-tech and covered in mirrors. He really needed to get to the gym and tone up his six pack which now looked more like a bulging sack of potatoes. Once Felix was dressed, that which came with laziness, age and lack of exercise was well hidden. He was looking forward to the evening and the meal. He loved meeting new people and thought he might just recruit some more contacts too. He began to rehearse what he might say to Stephen Baxter after the meal. He had to be pitch perfect as this deal could make or break him. He believed that the whole of the deal rested upon this one evening and nothing could go wrong. The signing of the contract would make a huge difference to his career and his impending retirement.

A knock on the door took Felix out of his egotistical blurb and he opened it to see Danny dressed in a blue butler outfit. "Are you ready, sir? I am to take you to the orangery."

"Yes of course, Danny, thank you." On the way down the corridors of this exquisite mansion Felix chatted with Danny. "So, you double up then?"

Danny took a short bow. "Yes sir, and I am the maintenance too." Felix followed Danny down a split regal staircase that ended on a white and gold marble floor. A few minutes later he was standing alone with a large mojito and trying to think where the oranges were, or why else would it be called an orangery? It wasn't long before the penny dropped, and orangery was just a posh word for big conservatory. Lots of people had conservatories but not everybody could afford a big conservatory called an orangery. Felix found a large armchair and sat back to enjoy the silence which was soon broken by Stephen Baxter.

"So sorry we were out when you arrived! I do hope that my people have been looking after you?" Felix took the hand of this rather distinguished looking man with receding hair that suited him and gold-rimmed glasses that were an adornment to his handsome face. The strong grip of Stephen Baxter nearly broke his fingers and Felix knew this man was not one to be messed with.

Danny appeared from nowhere and Stephen Baxter smiled. "I'll have what he's having Danny Boy, thank you. By the way what are you drinking Felix?" While they sipped their drinks the two men exchanged superficial pleasantries. "I must leave you now Felix to greet my guests. My mother-in-law will be joining us tonight, she is from your part of the world; somewhere in England. Remind me to show you the gardens before you leave in the morning." With that, the chief administrator of the FAA was gone.

It wasn't long before the orangery was full of an eclectic mix of people, ranging from politicians to film stars. Felix was in awe of where he was and began chatting to them all as he made his way around the room. He was never backward in coming forward. There were a few single women too and he wondered if he might get lucky.

Danny entered the room, banged a gong and announced that dinner was to be served. The crowd began to shuffle into the dining room. People were finding their names and places before sitting to eat. Felix found himself at the furthest end of the palatial room with one chair beside him empty and also the one directly opposite him. Just as he was going to look at the names of the two people who were missing, Stephen Baxter rose to give a toast. "Let us make a toast to posterity and prosperity and I apologise for the lateness of my wife and her mother, they never can make it on time. You know what women are like!" The guests laughed politely. Stephen asked Danny to serve more drinks while they waited.

Felix busied himself with the woman sitting next to him. Melody was a fashion editor with a popular woman's magazine, called 'Women just do it!' She was telling him about the book she was just about to have published, *Fanny by Day, Yoni by Night*. She was passionate about it and Felix listened intently to the southern Carolina drawl. "Well, you see Felix, Mummy wasn't best pleased when I told her that whilst I wasn't a lesbian, I did like women too. The title came from our conversation. I was telling her about tantric sex. Oh, don't look at me like that Felix, I love to shock my mother. She is an old southern lady who needs to get a life."

Felix laughed, "Why how am I looking at you?"

Melody wasn't pleased. "Well, I think you are looking at me rather judgmentally or is that just your shocked face?"

"Melody, let me tell you that nothing can shock me. So, what is your book about?" Melody went on to tell Felix that her book was about the attitude down the ages to the woman's vagina and how men had such a

27

hard time when women reclaimed their vaginas during the feminist movement.

"It goes way back to the writing of *Fanny Hill* a woman of pleasure and beyond, then comes right up to the present day and how women's concept of their vaginas has changed. Well men's too." Felix summoned Danny and asked if they might have more drinks.

"I read *Fanny Hill* when I was a young boy and *Lady Chatterley's Lover* too." Melody waited for Danny to pour their drinks before continuing.

"Did you know that *Fanny Hill* was written in seventeen forty-eight, and was banned more than any other book?" Felix was becoming bored now.

"No. So what else is there in your book, tell me the chapters."

"Oh, Felix. I can tell I am boring you." Melody looked into his eyes before slowly running her hand across his leg to find his man bits. He thought perhaps that he might not be spending a lonely night in his big bed after all. She continued to be lascivious, and he was loving it. So much so that he didn't notice the two women who entered the room; one sitting down beside him and one opposite. He was too far gone in his thoughts about getting into Melody's knickers later, that was if she was wearing any He decided that he would not kick Melody out of bed and was looking forward to tasting her favours

"Hello Felix." The voice dampened his fun as he turned to look at the woman now sitting next to him. This woman was elegantly dressed in green taffeta. He wondered how she knew his name. He didn't have time to reply when the woman who was now occupying the empty seat opposite spoke.

"We meet again Felix!" The woman opposite was an older version of the woman in green sitting beside him. The woman opposite had far too many wrinkles to be attractive but her hair was a magnificent shade of white and, piled high on top of her head, she looked rather regal. Just as he was about to speak, Felix felt a hand run up the inside of his thigh.

He thought, 'Not now Melody!' as his middle leg moved. Melody was trying to say that he could have her later but Felix's thoughts were now elsewhere as he tried to remember who the two women were.

As Felix was trying to get his thoughts into some kind of order, Stephen Baxter rose from his chair. "Well, here they are at last, please raise your glasses to my beautiful wife, Barbara, and her mother, Enid."

Danny and Diana began to serve dinner. Felix was rifling through his mind to see where these women might know him from. He looked across at the older woman. "I am sorry, but do I know you?" Surely this old woman could not have been one of his conquests? He couldn't remember the younger one either.

Enid looked at her daughter. "Well, I suppose it has been a long time, but I never thought he'd forget these two lasses from Lancashire." Barbara did not speak, and the dinner continued with a certain normality, with course upon course gracing the table.

Melody whispered, "Shall we get together later?" Felix affirmed with a nod and a wink. It wasn't until they were all tucking in to the cheese and biscuits that he began to feel very uncomfortable as a memory began to reawaken. Oh no, this was a part of his past he would rather forget altogether but there was no escaping it now as it was sitting beside him and across from him. He remembered Adam's words.

CHAPTER THREE

Felix's memory returned rather quickly and he remembered. Here it was the past once more rearing its ugly head.

It was Felix's lucky day when the hostess on a long-haul flight became ill and Barbara, who had only been on the job six weeks, was called in to replace her. Barbara was a very pretty, redhead. She was twenty-two going on sixteen and it wasn't long before she fell for the charms of the older Felix. He'd had his eye on her since the interview and what she lacked in qualifications she made up for in enthusiasm.

The day they both stepped onto the airbus, Felix carried on his grooming techniques and ignored the smirks of the other hostesses. Barbara was besotted by Felix and his powerful position. It wasn't long before she became an initiate of the 'mile high' club. The whole event went badly wrong when Felix was pushing his way into her. A tap snapped on the small sink where she was perched and began to spray everywhere.

The stopover in Dubai was almost perfect, had not an interested tourist staying at the same hotel asked Barbara what her father did for a living. "Oh, he's not my father he's my…" She turned to Felix for the answer.

Without thinking Felix replied, "I'm her boyfriend." The tourist smiled one of those 'of course you are' smiles and walked away.

Barbara began to blush as she asked, "Are you really my boyfriend or were you just saying that?" Felix did not reply and asked Barbara if she would like another drink.

That night Barbara confided in Felix that he was her first. He was stunned as she hadn't been as tight as most virgins, and he mentioned this point to her. After another bottle of house wine (Felix didn't need to impress this one), Barbara revealed the reason she was not tight. "I read this book; you see. Most of my friends lost their virginity when they were sixteen when it became legal and I thought I would save myself for someone special, like you." Felix began to feel something akin to panic or perhaps it might have been anxiety. Barbara, who was more than tipsy now went on to say, "I love you Felix, I have loved you since the first day I saw you." His anxiety was now bordering on fear. He had a feeling that this one might complicate his life. Putting his fear aside he asked her what the book said. He was genuinely interested.

"It was a manual for women who had problems with tight vaginas and such like. It wasn't for men. It gave lots of practical advice."

Felix really wanted to know more. "Like what?"

Barbara giggled. "Well, it gave a list of things that could be a substitute for the man thingy. Oh, I can't say Felix." She giggled again.

"Yes, you can, I am broad-minded and won't tell anyone." Barbara went on to tell him that she had experimented with vibrators but found the closest thing to a man's penis (the book said) was a courgette.

"Do you mean a zucchini?"

"No Felix I mean a courgette!"

Sometimes Felix despaired of her. "You did it with a courgette?"

"Yes, I did, and I had my first orgasm." Felix didn't know whether to laugh or cry. So, a vegetable was up Barbara's love tunnel way before him! Well, Felix thought, 'This one has surprised me, and she might be up for anything.' A few hours later they were practically swinging from the chandelier in the bedroom and sex gymnastics were taken to another level.

On their return to England Felix tried to cool off the relationship but Barbara began to stalk him. His only way to escape her attention was to keep himself away from the airport and he was lucky that it was the time of year that he took tour operators abroad on working trips courtesy of his airline. He soon forgot about Barbara after having a good time in some of the cities in Europe. It wasn't until nearly Christmas when he returned to his office to find a note on his desk from the stalking Barbara. 'Felix, I must see you, it is more than important.'

That afternoon they were sitting across from each other in public view in the departure lounge at Manchester airport. She began to cry and Felix thought that perhaps they ought to be more private so he guided her to the cleaning cupboard on the third floor. Barbara told him that she was pregnant and that it was his. Felix took his mounting anger out on the floor as he paced up and down. "I thought you were on the pill, I thought that all hostesses were?"

Barbara felt her anger mounting now too. "You pig Felix! So, you mean you believe that we all sleep around? You were my first."

He couldn't help himself. "Ha, you mean after an array of vegetables." He realised that perhaps he had overstepped the mark and took Barbara's hand. He led her to a pile of boxes and sat her down.

She looked up at him with pleading eyes. "What are we going to do?" All he could think was that she would have been better served reading a book on birth control and not one telling her to fuck herself with a zucchini.

"We are going to my office right now, dry your tears and come on." Once sitting behind his desk Felix felt some kind of order return to his thoughts and he took a small blue card out of the drawer. "A man in my position can't have anything like this going on in his life and there is no 'we'!" He put emphasis on the 'we'. "You haven't told anyone have you?"

Barbara hesitated. "No, but I think my mother suspects something." Felix pushed the blue card across the desk.

"Ring this number, I will take care of everything and tell no one."

Barbara was ashen and Felix felt a twinge of guilt but there was no way he could have his reputation sullied by an unwanted child. "Come sit down on the sofa," he said as he got her a glass of water. A patronizing tone ran through the next thing he said. "Please understand there was no 'we' and there is no 'us. What we did was for two consenting adults having some fun with their bodies, that is all."

"But I love you, Felix."

He sighed. "No, you don't, you don't even know me. Now be a good girl and toddle off and ring that number."

Felix never saw Barbara again. He did, however, see her mother, Enid, a few weeks later. There was a commotion outside his office and he heard raised voices. He heard his secretary calmly saying, "I am so sorry, but you cannot go in without an appointment."

"Oh, can't I?" Enid screamed. "Watch this, madam." She burst through the door like a mad woman trying to escape an asylum. The secretary followed. Enid turned on her. "If you know what's good for you lady, get out! Get out now!" The secretary left closing the door behind her. Felix rose from his chair. Enid was now in full battle mode and gave the balding man before her, the one who had marred her daughter, the dead eye. Her rage was insurmountable. "Sit down now," she said to a bewildered Felix. He obeyed as he could see that this woman was not to be argued with.

There was a moment's pause before Enid placed herself across the desk from Felix and she looked down on this man; a rat of the worst kind. With hands on her hips in true Lancashire angry woman fashion, Enid began.

"Well, mister big airline man, so you think you can deflower my only child? You knock her up and then want to send her to an abortionist? What fucking planet have you come from? Well let me tell you, you will never ever see her again. She has left the country now and I am on the next plane out of here too. She needs to get a new life and I will make sure she does." Enid walked round the desk and put her face close to Felix's. Enid very slowly and menacingly said, "I am telling you this, Felix, pray that we never, ever, meet again as that might be your undoing. Be afraid, be very afraid."

Enid was on the next flight to Washington. Felix sat for a while and tried to understand what had just happened. Well, the mother was upset about the abortion, but it was for the best and Barbara was young, she would have other children. The mother probably hadn't had a man for years and was frustrated, why else would someone behave like a screaming banshee? Hadn't he read somewhere that anger was like an aphrodisiac? It gets blood flowing. The heart rate and blood pressure go up and it increases testosterone levels. This was all linked to sexual arousal. He turned to the papers on his desk and soon Barbara and her mother were long gone from his thoughts never to be remembered again, until now.

CHAPTER FOUR

As Danny refilled his glass Felix felt his angst growing as he remembered the happenings of twenty years before. He wondered if he should make his excuses and leave. He needed that contract so much, that it wasn't really an option. He hoped that Stephen Baxter knew nothing. He couldn't know as Felix wouldn't be there at his table, would he? He soon got his answer when Stephen stood up, tapped his glass and called for order in the room. "I won't take long but would like to introduce you to our guest from England. Mr Felix Schwarz. He is from the same part of England as my wife and her mother. I met my wife ten years ago after she started working for American Airlines in the sales office. It was love at first sight and it wasn't long before we were married. Down the years she has made me so happy, and my continuing success is due to having her beside me. They say behind every successful man there is a good woman. I have been blessed by having two good women and ask that you please raise your glasses to Barbara and Enid, my English queens."

After all the guests left, Stephen Baxter and Felix enjoyed a rare cognac in the study; a rather large man cave which was next to the orangery. They were discussing the contract. "Felix, everything is in order and my lawyers are just finalising details. We have done a great deal and the work you have put into this is much appreciated. The final documents will be ready Monday. We will both benefit from this great arrangement." Felix felt rather warm and smug.

"Thank you, sir. I know you won't be disappointed."

They sat together in silence watching the dying embers of a fire that was about to expire when there was a knock at the door. Enid entered followed by a young man who looked to be in his late teens. Stephen rose and gave the boy a hug. "You want to join us, boy?" he asked. Enid turned to leave but not before she gave Felix a sideways glance. It was an all-knowing smirk of satisfaction.

She closed the door behind her as Felix thought, 'Fucking witch.' Stephen continued to speak.

"Let me introduce you to my new English friend, Felix." He turned to Felix. "This is my son, Mark, how do you say it in England? The apple of my eye?" Mark and Felix shook hands and Mark turned to his father.

"I need to pack so can't join you now as we are off early. So, it's OK that Joseph comes up to the cabin with us Dad? We could do with some fun in the Rockies. I only have two weeks left before uni."

Stephen lit a big cigar before saying, "Yes, of course son and I have arranged for Malcolm to fly you all up there. We can discuss details before you leave tomorrow, it's been a long day." Mark bent down and kissed his father on the forehead.

He turned to Felix. "It was good to meet you Felix, maybe we will meet again someday."

Stephen asked Felix if he had children. "No, it was never meant to be. My wife lost a few and it took its toll on her health." What Felix meant was that his wife began to prefer alcohol instead of him and their relationship was dead in the water. "You've got a nice lad there, Stephen." Stephen took a large puff on the tobacco stick.

"I certainly do. He's not really mine, you know. He is my only son though as me and my first wife couldn't have children. Turned out to be my fault, the lazy fish weren't swimming. She left me and now has six kids. Six, imagine that!"

Felix was feeling tired. "Oh, I see." Stephen went on.

"When I met Barbara, she had the boy. She told me that she was a widow and I adopted him. She couldn't have any more, so he is very precious to us both."

Stephen refilled their glasses. "It's strange really because she would never talk about the father, don't even know his name. She said he was a wastrel, and it didn't matter as he was dead now and not worth a breath. I don't know how or why he died. I respect her too much to go there and it doesn't really matter. That boy, Felix, that boy and his mother have brought me more joy and happiness than I could have imagined." Stephen fell silent and soon he was sleeping in his maroon leather-winged chair, the fire out now. Felix drained his glass before he quietly left the room. He looked around for the lovely Melody only to by Danny that she left with an actress from Mexico.

That night Felix had a nightmare, something he didn't often do. It was more like a psychedelic trip than a bad dream. Faces were flashing in and out of a red cloud that burst and rained blood. He could hear a woman crying and an angry voice shouting at him. He was in a large white room and he slipped and fell on the floor. He'd stood on a placenta and now his hands were covered in blood. A baby began to cry, and Felix woke up with a start to find he'd wet the bed. After a quick shower and a turn of the mattress Felix opened the window and looked out at a waning moon. The declining moon looked sad and Felix was glad that he would be leaving the Alpines in the morning.

Felix was eager to tell Adam that he'd pulled the deal off and a few weeks later they went clubbing. They weren't alone, as Felix hired two escorts that giggled a lot. They looked good on the arm but weren't very good at stimulating conversation. In fact, they were rather boring and spent most of the night chatting between themselves, and to Felix. Adam felt left out but he didn't mind. He had much to think about.

During the evening, Adam disappeared for about half an hour. When he returned, he didn't seem in a good frame of mind. He made his excuses and left for the hotel. "I might not catch you in the morning Felix so have a good flight home and all the best." They gave each other a man hug and Adam left Felix to his plans for a night of debauchery with the two gigglers.

CHAPTER FIVE

Monday morning and Felix was back at Manchester airport. He had spent his last few days in America looking at properties to buy and partying with Adam. He'd managed to get another session in with Ling and Lang. This time Adam was not with him, and things got out of hand as Shu Fang also joined in. All thoughts of Barbara and Enid were gone from his mind as he looked forward to a beautiful future and his eventual new life somewhere else. His secretary did not turn up for work the following morning, so Felix busied himself opening the post and sorting his emails when there was a knock on his door. He went to open it and was greeted by Simon, his boss.

"Simon, I thought you were away in Germany this week?"

"Yes, I am off this afternoon but had to stay on this morning to tie up some loose ends."

"Coffee, Simon?" Simon shook his head and Felix syphoned himself some water before sitting down at his desk. "How can I help you?" he asked.

Felix noticed that Simon looked rather uncomfortable. As the atmosphere began to thicken, Felix became aware of unsaid words running up the walls and needed to break the awkward silence.

"Is everything OK, Simon, with the deal?"

"Oh yes, Felix, it's all good. You did a brilliant job and Stephen Baxter is flying over next week." Felix felt relieved.

"It will be a cause for a celebration. Do you want me to organise something?"

Simon gave a half smile. "No, it is OK, we have it all in hand, thanks. As I said, you did an awesome job. We've been after that contract for years and you pulled it off. I think I will have that drink now. Black coffee, no sugar!"

Felix picked up the phone and it wasn't long before they were drinking coffees brought in by Janet, Felix's new interest. He hadn't noticed the large manilla envelope that Simon had with him until it was pushed across the desk towards him. "What's this then?" He opened it with the excitement of a child believing it to be the bonus that he was promised if he managed to bag the contract. Indeed, it was. The top page was thanking him and stated that his reward would be in his bank by the end of the month. He looked up at Simon. "This is more than we agreed, has there been a mistake?"

"No mistake, the board felt you more than deserved it." A big grin spread across his face as he thanked his boss.

Felix was about to put the paperwork into the drawer when Simon said, "I think you need to read it all now Felix." Felix turned the page and took his time, feeling that his heart was about to beat out of his chest. The paperwork was laying out the terms of his dismissal, politely termed as early retirement.

"Simon, I don't understand? Retirement? I have another ten years left in me and I have already taken out a lease on an apartment in Manhattan. I was told before I went that if I pulled this off, I could run the operation over there."

Felix wasn't feeling very confident when he said, "Simon this was a major coup." Simon finished his coffee before saying, "Yes indeed, the last one with us. Look Felix, there's no way to say this. We have known each other for years and although I shouldn't be telling you, I feel as your friend I owe you that much. After you left America, Stephen Baxter spoke to our CEO in Cologne. He told him that he would not invoke the fourteen days withdrawal from the contract and would continue with the agreement only if you were no longer with us. The contract is bigger than an employee, Felix. You should understand this."

"But why I don't understand, Stephen and I got on so well?" Felix had no intention of telling anything about the past with Baxter's wife. He felt the bottom slowly sliding out of his world.

"We have no idea why. Stephen Baxter didn't say. But he did make it clear that if you were to remain with the company the deal was off. We have been very generous with your package as we doubt you will get another job with an airline now. Time to think about retiring maybe? He is more than a powerful man. I don't know what you did and don't want to know. It is as it is, mate and I am so sorry."

"Simon, I don't know what to say."

"There is nothing to say." Felix felt the rug being pulled from under him.

"Shall I leave at the end of the month?"

Simon hated what he was doing. "No."

Felix slumped in his chair. "Not the end of the week?"

Simon was concerned as Felix began to look unwell. "No, I am sorry, but you must pack your things and leave now."

Two hours later with his blood pressure pounding and hurting his brain Felix left Manchester airport never to return. He didn't take another job and retired to his barge on the canal at Llangollen. It was a few years later while he was watching the news on his TV that he caught a feature about the youngest ever American standing for Congress. The name Mark Baxter caught his attention. As Mark looked towards the camera smiled and waved, Felix looked at a reflection of himself when he was in his twenties.

Felix had many moments whilst on the canal to reflect on his life after he rang Barbara, who confirmed that Mark Baxter was indeed his son. He had to tell someone, and he rang Adam. Adam listened with disbelief, and it was a good thing that Felix couldn't see him as he was smiling. "Well Felix it looks like you have had some home truths and what I said to you in New York happened. You got your comeuppance and now you have to live with all that you have done." Felix thought that Adam was being rather harsh but said nothing. "Why don't you call in and see me if you are passing? You will love my boat." Adam said he would. He had no intentions of seeing Felix ever again. He could never forget how he spoke about his night with Olivia in Hamburg. The man was disgusting!

CHAPTER SIX

It was early morning and Olivia made her way out towards the arrivals lounge. She was so tired. Her sombre mood did not stop her smiling. It was quite a night flight, which was now fast becoming a memory. It was something to file in her mind and perhaps look at later or maybe never! The flight from Manchester was a memorable one, never to be forgotten. Now all Olivia wanted to do was to forget it.

Memories stick and won't go away, or they run and hide in a secret inaccessible place never to return. She couldn't decide if she had a double 'A' time on the flight; was it awful or awesome? One thing for sure was that some of the things she thought she had dealt with all those years ago hadn't been dealt with at all. Was it a coincidence or something else?

What Olivia didn't need was her past coming back to haunt her. She had dealt with those demons a long time ago and now they had resurfaced, and she wasn't sure why. Those who hurt her the most were accountable for their behaviours and she too was accountable for hers. Those behaviours were to map the rest of her life and she was stronger for them and more resilient. That did not stop the armour sometimes having a hole in it and allowing others into her world, her sacred space.

Olivia looked at the card in her hand and thrust it deep into her pocket. She turned her back on her past and walked away. Her mind telling her, "Walk away, keep walking, do not turn around, that was then and this is now. He will only hurt you again and there is a future and tomorrow waiting round the corner. There is no point in going back.'

She did not turn around to look back at Adam as she walked away from him and the pain she felt. There was no point and she hoped that he too was suffering. She knew it was the right thing to do and yet her heart was screaming, 'Go back, you know you want to, turn around and go back, he is waiting. You loved him once, you can love him again. Do you still love him? Did you ever really get over him?' She took a deep breath and carried on walking. Fighting back the tears she walked out of the airport and onto the street to be confronted by a sea of faces all looking for someone. She saw Felix climbing into the back of a cream Cadillac. She scowled as she thought of his apology and the tears left on the plane. She smiled as she hoped that one day, he might get his comeuppance.

Olivia searched the wave of faces before her and eventually saw a card with her name on. It was held high, by a rather beautiful looking woman who could have been of mixed race. The young woman waved at her. She reminded Olivia of a young Buffy St Marie, who sang the title song to one of Olivia's all-time favourite films, *Soldier Blue*. Olivia smiled and began to walk towards the woman as a memory flooded her mind.

Soldier Blue was released in 1970 when Olivia was still a teenager. It was a film of comedy, love, idiocy and showed what happened to the Native Americans at the Sandy Creek Massacre in 1864. Olivia would drive her friends mad by playing the song over and over again. She felt an affiliation to the Native Americans even though she had never met one. The song touched her heart and sometimes she cried. When she got drunk at the end of a party night, Olivia would place the vinyl on the turntable and her friends would know that it was time to leave. The party would be over.

The young woman spoke, "Olivia? Is it Olivia?"

"Yes, it is," replied Olivia. "And may I ask who you are, please?"

"Manaba Maluka Fast Thunder."

Olivia was right. This beautiful woman before her was Native American. They smiled at each other and as their eyes met, they knew they were going to become friends.

"Would you mind calling me Marcia? It is easier." Olivia nodded and Marcia continued. "I am your shadow, Your PA, your best friend while you are here. Anything you want I shall get for you."

Olivia yawned as she spoke, "Right now I am so tired I could sleep for a week."

Marcia took Olivia by the arm, guiding her through the myriads of people all trying to get to the same cab. Olivia turned her head once to look back the way she came. Was she hoping to catch a glimpse of Adam? How would she have felt if she saw him amongst the sea of faces? Too many faces met her tired eyes and she turned to walk with Marcia. The voice in her head began to chastise her, 'Don't look back! Walk forward to your future!'

They pushed their way through the waiting crowd and came to the edge of the pavement where Marcia hailed a cab. As they settled the cabby asked, "You mind if I play the music girls?" Without waiting for an answer, he switched his Bluetooth on, and Olivia could not believe her ears.

"Who is singing this?"

The cabbie sounded surprised. "It is Gabrielle. Brilliant song I think 'Closure' is one of her best."

Olivia closed her eyes and fought the tears. As the song came to an end, she had to pull herself together and she turned to Marcia. "You have a beautiful name, has it got meaning?"

Marcia smiled. "Thank you. Manaba means 'war returned with her coming'. Maluka means 'Sunny Day' and Fast Thunder speaks for itself."

Olivia looked out of the window to see a rainbow fading fast. "You are Lakota Sioux then?" Marcia nodded.

"Olivia, do you know about the Indians?"

"Not as much as I would like to. I have read a lot of books and it is so sad what happened to the Native Americans. Such an injustice! You are the first one I have met."

"My mother is Cheyenne and my father a Lakota Sioux." Marcia went on to tell Olivia all about her family and their history.

They chatted all the way into the city; seventeen miles of words that were lulling Olivia to sleep. Marcia did most of the talking as Olivia's mind began to wander. She was still running with the events of the past hours since leaving Manchester. The journey into the city took forever, as the traffic danced along the road. Stop, go, stop, go!

Eventually they pulled up in front of the Trump International Hotel. Olivia looked up at the imposing structure.

"Am I staying here?"

Marcia answered, "Of course, why not?"

Olivia laughed. "Do you know what trump means in Yorkshire? It means fart. I am staying at the Fart International. I bet it's full of old farts."

Marcia didn't comment. In fact, her face told Olivia that her joke had just gone over the top of her head. Did the Americans not have the same sense of humour? Of course, they must, as Olivia's favourite comedian was Robin Williams. She never missed an episode of *Mork and Mindy*. Nanu! Nanu!

Perhaps Americans don't talk about bodily functions? Olivia made a note to self to be more careful with the things she said. That might be hard for her as she sometimes spoke before her brain engaged.

As the door to the cab opened, Olivia was greeted by 'Ace Face' from the film *Quadrophenia*. He was a young Sting lookalike. "Have you any cases in the back, mam?" Olivia nodded and she turned to Marcia.

"Do you mind if I go in alone, please? I don't mean to be rude, but I am whacked."

Marcia smiled as she thrust a green file into Olivia's hand.

"It's all there, the itinerary, the details, everything you need. I will call you tomorrow. OK?"

Olivia smiled a tired smile. "Thank you, Marcia, I think you and I are going to get along very well indeed."

Ace Face was back and holding his hand out to Olivia. He helped her out of the cab. Marcia waved as the cab moved away. She soon became a yellow blob amongst all the other yellow blobs going in the same direction. Olivia turned and followed the young bellboy into an imposing reception hall. The marble floors and wood panelled walls had money written all over them. Check in didn't take too long and soon Olivia was in the lift going up. Ace Face pressed the number ten.

When they arrived at the Park View Executive suite Olivia asked Ace Face what his name was. "Gordon, mam, but most people call me Gordy."

She replied, "Then Gordy it is." (Although secretly she wanted to call him Sting.) Olivia placed ten dollars in his palm.

"Thank you, mam. Can I get you anything? If you need anything at all ask for me."

"No thank you Gordy and yes I will. That will be all for now, goodnight!"

Olivia looked around. This wasn't a hotel room; it was an apartment. Olivia went into the kitchen and looked in the fridge. It was stocked with all sorts of goodies. She heated up some milk and added sugar. Olivia began a quick exploration of her environment, the place that would be home for her, now. There were more windows than walls. To the left she could see Central Park and the lights of the city twinkling on the horizon. As she looked down to the right, she saw lights of the cars travelling around the Columbus Circle. They looked like ants carrying torches. In the stillness of her space, she felt the life in the city below.

Olivia sat on the edge of the bed drinking her hot milk. It was the one thing that would help her sleep and she was finding it hard to switch her brain off. None of this seemed real. It was hard to believe that a few years ago she was writing a book at her kitchen table. It was almost autobiographical with added bits. Then on the plane coming over, so high in the sky, she saw the man she loved all those years ago sitting next to a man who hurt her beyond words. To be honest, she acknowledged that they both hurt her. She wasn't going to think about that now, she was too tired. Olivia lay down on the bed. She would unpack in the morning. She soon fell into a deep sleep. As her subconscious tried to make sense of all that transpired on the plane. Olivia dreamt of a past that was now merging with her future. Why were they all on the same plane together? Would she ever know?

In the morning she felt rather disorientated. A phone was ringing somewhere. Olivia opened her eyes for a moment, forgetting where she was. The phone stopped. She slowly made her way to the bathroom. It was an amazing bathroom with a jacuzzi bath and gold accessories. This was all so very posh and sterile. She wasn't used to this opulence and felt that she really should not be somewhere so grand. Olivia looked in the mirror, her hair all over the place and her face ravaged by the stress of yesterday. As she ran the bath, she heard a knock on the door. Opening it she found Gordy hiding behind a massive bunch of sunflowers and lilacs. He also had a silver bucket.

"Morning, mam, hope you slept well?" He was far too cheerful.

"Yes, Gordy I did. Are you sure these are for me?"

Gordy looked at the card. "Is your name Olivia Orphanidis?"

Olivia nodded. "Then they are for you, mam."

"You better put them over there on the table then."

Gordy added, "The champagne is courtesy of the management." Olivia thanked Gordy. As he left the room he called, "Have a nice day, mam."

Olivia took the card from the flowers, poured herself a glass of champagne, went across to the bathroom and stepped into the warm, inviting jacuzzi. She looked at the card. There was no message, only her name. Strange! Who would send flowers and not put a message on? She took a large gulp of her drink and switched on the jacuzzi. Olivia lost herself in the bubbles and began to drift off to the music from a South Carolina Beach radio station that was blaring from her laptop. She soon forgot about the mystery of the flowers and wallowed in the essence of roses that floated around her.

Wrapped in a big white fluffy robe, Olivia answered the phone that had rung more than once while she indulged herself in the bathroom. It was Marcia. Olivia wondered how Marcia could say so much without taking a breath. Eventually she was able to speak. "Yes, I will be ready." She put the phone down and hurriedly unpacked her bags.

Half an hour later Olivia was downstairs waiting for Marcia. Thus began an endless stream of interviews, fancy dinners and non-stop talking. The high life was good for a short time, but it began to wear Olivia down. The heavy workload was taking its toll and she didn't care if she never saw the inside of a yellow taxicab ever again. After yet another dinner she looked in the mirror at a tired drawn face that couldn't possibly be hers. "Come on girl get a grip. Learn to say NO! This is your life."

Olivia needed some discipline. She wasn't getting to bed till two or three most mornings; the clubs were too enticing and she forgot her age. She was becoming bored with clubbing and shopping, which occurred in the gaps between official book stuff. This was extra to all the book signings and interviews she was also attending.

Olivia was beginning to understand that New York never sleeps and neither do some of the people in it. It wasn't like rural Yorkshire that closed down every night. It was easy to get on the roller coaster of a glitz and glamour life. It was not that easy to get off it. It never stopped moving. It slowed down sometimes but it never stopped moving. Her tired, drawn pale face with purple bags hanging down under her eyes was speaking volumes. It said, 'Stop now!'

After a particularly hectic day and night when things did not go right and were very frustrating, Olivia made a mental note to speak to Marcia about taking some time off to re-energize. She would do this in the morning. As she crawled into bed, she looked at the clock. Oh goodness, it was morning! Normal people were just getting up to go to work and she was just getting into bed.

Olivia had to take control of what was happening to her. She pulled the quilt tightly around herself and found sanctuary in the giant bed where she could reflect upon another awesome day in the Big Apple. Before the sandman came, Olivia managed to say her three 'gratefuls' which had taken the place of prayers a few months earlier.

Her first book was going viral, which was an awesome feeling. So, she used the 'gratefuls' as a means of saying a big thank you to God. She rarely asked for anything as she was now creating her own destiny. It was pointless relying on a deity that gave her choices. This was her life, her choices and her learning pathway. What happens to a person is down to them, not some God in the sky or wherever.

Olivia felt that God was a very personal thing and each person had their own views. She never talked about her God to anyone. Her three 'gratefuls' were repetitious as she was always grateful for the same things, although sometimes they changed a little. After reciting grateful for my health and good fortune, grateful for that yellow cab missing me today, grateful for the good weather, she added a quick, "Please get me out of here, now. I have had enough."

Olivia knew how lucky she was. She had created her future, sitting in her little house in Yorkshire. She created a heroine that told a story of her past. Olivia fulfilled her lifelong dream to write a book. She had come so far and become the heroine in her own adventure. She was now the master of her future.

It wasn't long before Olivia was snoring, and the raging storm began. The banging on the windows was unbelievable. The rain lashed down and the winds served to clean the streets and make way for another sunny day.

The bad weather eventually moved on and Olivia rose after a dreamless sleep. As she sat sipping her morning coffee she thought back to when she first arrived at Fart's Hotel. She'd found the opulence rather intimidating. That first night she just stared at everything and dare not sit down. She felt totally out of her depth, and it was a little frightening. She was now sitting on the gold and purple chaise longue, smiling at her initial reaction to such grandeur. It had not taken her long to reach a comfortable zone and lose her awe.

The suite on floor ten was now a second home to her.
Olivia smiled as she remembered the boy from room service who brought her breakfast that same day and watched her touching everything. She laughed when she saw his face.

"Are you all right, mam?"

"I really don't know."

The boy's name was Harvey. Olivia always made a point of asking who she was talking to. Harvey wasn't too sure why Olivia was laughing. He hadn't met many people from Yorkshire. Although, last year a butcher from Castleford, who had won the lottery, stayed at the hotel. Harvey couldn't remember his name but remembered that he used to say a lot, "There's 'nowt', so queer as folk, young un." The man would say this as he gave him a tip. Although he had lots of money, the man from Castleford was mean with his tips.

Harvey couldn't really understand the man and now he wondered if the man might know this smiley woman who laughed a lot. Maybe the butcher meant her? Was she a 'queer folk'? She too always had a smile. Harvey wondered if she was poor, as his experience was that rich people didn't smile much and were rather rude. Whereas this lady always had a kind word for him.

That day had been long and tiring and Olivia was remembering this as Harvey left the room after bringing her a supper of antipasto and fresh bread. It was past midnight as Olivia poured herself a glass of wine and answered the phone.

"Who is calling me at this hour?"

A slurry American, chocolate flavoured, voice answered. "It's me, Marcia, did I wake you?"

"Just having some supper and then I am off to bed."

Marcia went on. "I know you are getting tired. I watched you today, it has been a long week for you."

"You could say that".

"That." They, both laughed. They were fast becoming best buddies and it helped to have the same sense of humour.

"OK. I have been looking at the calendar and have managed to do some juggling so you can have some leisure time." Why did Marcia always have to tell Olivia things that could wait till they next met? Surely this could have waited till later? Olivia's English politeness tied her tongue down and she carried on listening.

"Listen up, Olivia. Tomorrow morning you have a hair appointment at seven with John Barrett at Bergdorf Goodman, followed at eleven by a meeting at Atlantic TV. They want to do a half hour slot on you when you return from Los Angeles. We might be able to grab a bagel or something during the morning. We should be done by twelve thirty and then you are free till Tuesday afternoon. How does that grab you, my dear?"

If Marcia had been in the room Olivia would have grabbed her and kissed her. She was beginning to love this woman who was so good at her job, made sure everything ran smoothly and was well tuned in to Olivia's needs. "So dear, you can decide what you would like to do, and I can make it happen."

Marcia stopped for breath and was silent waiting for Olivia to reply. "Yes tomorrow, please not now... later. I will think about it, goodnight love." Olivia sighed as she replaced the phone.

Marcia was a magician. Well sort of was, but not quite. She couldn't do everything. She was not able to trace who sent the flowers when Olivia arrived at the hotel. She was unable to wave her magic wand on that one. Olivia looked at the clock knowing that in less than four hours Marcia would be banging on her door. She took her drink to bed and thought about the past few days. Olivia was still coming to terms with how rapidly her life had changed. How she was whisked away from the Yorkshire Moors, across the world to this alien environment.

She fell into a deep sleep and dreamt of red roses being thrown at her by someone she could not see. It wasn't the first time she had this dream since landing in America. The flowers were not always the same and, more often than not, there would be sunflowers and lilacs.

CHAPTER SEVEN

The following morning, as Olivia was sipping her espresso, she thought back to her first yellow cab ride on her own. It certainly was an experience of taxi travel, 'New York style'. The cabbie was called Aldo. He was of Italian, Polish descent. Aldo never stopped talking. When the car was not in motion his hands would leave the steering wheel and wave about dancing to his words in the air. Aldo was a welcome diversion from her thoughts as the disturbing flight from Manchester and the revelations on the plane left residue of her past. In her lone moments, her feelings for Felix and Adam were still with her. She really didn't want to think about them. She wanted to forget all of it. It took Aldo (who reminded her a little of Danny De Vito in *Taxi*) and his antics, to soon make her forget about the two men.

The tension she felt was broken when they became blocked in, up a 'one way' street and the traffic stopped moving. Time began to pass very slowly as five minutes turned into ten. Without warning Aldo jumped out of the cab and ran to the car in front. This one seemed to be causing the hold-up. Olivia wound her window down as Aldo began to shout profanities at an unseen human. "What the fuck you mean, it just stopped? Move it then!" Aldo began to jump up and down as he raged on the pavement.

Olivia couldn't help laughing as a young man took his phone out and began to film the action. She thought, 'Bet that will be on *You've Been Framed* next season or go viral on 'You Tube'. It wasn't long before the traffic began to move and Olivia reached her destination; her first book signing at The Strand. Aldo was to become her regular driver and they began a friendship of laughter and joviality.

Two days later Aldo dropped Olivia at a hairdresser's that she read about and wanted to try out. She was lucky that Marcia managed to get her a slot, as people waited weeks to grace the premises. Olivia loved going to the hairdressers as it was a welcome time of unwinding and rubbish chat.

"Coffee, would you like another coffee, mam?" The words of a twangy Bronx dialect hit Olivia's ear drums bringing her back to the present. Olivia looked at the mirror to see the face of a trendy young punk-looking thing, behind her. She was obviously one of the salon's juniors.

"No thank you, but some orange juice might be nice," Olivia replied. The stylist returned to put the finishing touches to Olivia's hair. Olivia loved the colour. She had gone back to blond. It would be much easier to manage with her roots not showing through as much now that she was actually quite white, naturally silver really. Olivia was not ready to let go to nature just yet. The style, however, was terrible and Olivia looked like a throwback from the eighties. That would never do!

Olivia looked at her stylist. "Your junior has gone to bring me some juice."

The tall flamboyant diva replied, "She 'ain't no junior, she the cleaner, she gets people's drinks to top up her pay with tips."

Olivia's wicked sense of humour came into play and she kept her thoughts to herself, that if anyone wanted a tip, Olivia would say, 'Well get a proper job then'. It would never do to say it out loud. When the cleaner returned Olivia slipped ten dollars into her hand.

The woman was very grateful. "Anything you want mam, anything, just ask for me."

Olivia knew what it was like to be poor, to live hand to mouth. It was only a few years before that her friends were bringing her bags of food as she fell on hard times. It was a time in her life she wished she could forget. A very humbling experience when she found out who her friends were.

As she sipped her juice Olivia began to compare New York to London, not that she had been to London much. London was like another planet, not at all like Yorkshire. It was full of people from different parts of the world. New York was in the same universe but in a different part of the galaxy. There were more people here, descendants from 'who knows where'. People all going somewhere, never having time to look up at the sun. Everywhere was busy, busy and busy.

Marcia was waiting for Olivia by the desk finishing a call on her cell phone. They didn't call them mobiles here. That was another thing Olivia noticed; they spoke the same language, but the Americans did not speak English. "Marcia, we need to stop by the hotel please." Olivia needed to do something with the expensive mess of hair. Marcia looked at her lime green Ice watch.

"OK, we can detour, you have fifteen minutes," she said as she walked towards the elevator. Olivia smiled. She had a new name for Marcia. She called her 'right arm'. She could not survive without her right arm and Marcia was fast becoming her American best friend.

Back at the hotel Olivia rifled through her suitcase to find her hair straighteners. No way was she going out looking like an ageing Krystle Carrington; the days of *Dynasty* were long gone. She took the first few messages from her phone while she waited for the hair appliance to heat up. First message was from Anne. Her chosen little sister began to babble about nothing, as usual!

Olivia caught the end of the message as Anne said, "So I am going to go blonder, I can have more blonde moments like that day you took me through the Mersey tunnel for the first time, do you remember? Oh! Better be off now someone just came into the shop. Hope you are enjoying yourself? You must be as I can never catch you in."

Anne was gone and Olivia smiled. Anne worked for a friend in a furniture shop in Ilkley. It was a posh little town with lots of quaint traditional shops. Business was always quiet and Anne spent most of her time on the phone, the internet or just cleaning the shop she had already cleaned. She was good at selling furniture to posh people with more money than sense and complained often that she was not busy enough.

Olivia smiled. She could never forget that blonde moment. She once took Anne through the Mersey tunnel in Liverpool and as they were driving down into the bowels of the earth Anne suddenly asked the question to end all questions. The funny part was that she was really serious. She said, "Olivia, do you think they put the tunnel here first and then the river over the top?"

Amazed, Olivia asked, "What?" It wasn't until Anne repeated her question that she realised what she had said and by the time they hit daylight they were laughing; in stitches. Tears were streaming down their faces as Olivia said, "I can't believe you just said that." They laughed all the way out of Liverpool. Once on the M62 Olivia said, "You know I so love you, Anne. All these years you have been there for me, through thick and thin, we have our secrets and now we are stuck to each other because we know too much." Anne gave her a conspiratorial look. It was a good memory and gave Olivia a warm feeling in her heart.

Olivia was missing her friend and wished she had come along. Anne was always busy these days looking after her grandchildren, their lives had forked in the road, but they were still as close as ever. Olivia promised Anne that if she ever got the book made into a film that Anne would walk the red carpet with her. She was sure there would be many more adventures with her bestie in the future.

The talks for the TV interview went very well, even though the producers thought that Olivia wanted to say too much about Yorkshire. Olivia thought it would be good to do some tourist promotion. Didn't they all like the Brontë sisters? They were writers too.

She was taken aback when the director asked, "Who?"

"One of them wrote *Wuthering Heights*, surely you have heard of that? There have been umpteen films made about it. The first one was made by Goldwyn. I can't believe you wouldn't know that! I live three miles from Haworth where they lived. There are always Americans there on holiday," she said.

Olivia didn't much like the director who had obviously not done his homework and was constantly looking at his watch. He had one of those faces that needed slapping hard. All he wanted to do was to talk about the sex in her book and he kept harping on about *Fifty Shades*. Olivia was beginning to get annoyed. "That was fifty shades of grey! My book is more like fifty-one shades of lavender. You cannot compare them."

She didn't often swear but when she left the building she turned to Marcia and said, "What a right twat he was."

Marcia asked, "What is a twat?"

Olivia blushed. "Well, it is used to call someone a fool."

Marcia replied, "Sounds a good word, maybe I shall use it."

Olivia panicked, "Err, no, not a good idea because it actually means vulva, female genitals."

"Oh!" came from Marcia. "I see." Olivia she should not have said it but the twat had really got her back up and was a time waster. The man was not a people person he was an egotist who thought only of himself and his career.

"Are you still going to walk round Central Park this afternoon?" Marcia asked.

"I certainly am, can't wait," Olivia said with excitement.

Taking a neatly folded sheet of paper from her pocket Marcia held it out and said, "Well you better take this then, and I will see you tomorrow afternoon be ready at two thirty." Olivia took the paper and put it in her coral suit pocket. She loved that suit. She wore it often and had travelled on the plane wearing it. It made her feel good and grown-up.

It didn't matter how old Olivia was she never quite felt grown-up. What did it mean anyway? The grown-up people she knew were boring and growing old far too quickly. She couldn't imagine ever being like that, she liked life too much and it was for living. She was going to live hers right to the end.

Olivia was creating her new destiny and, whilst the body ages, the mind can be in teenage state forever. A person has to be positive about things and not fear ageing as it is an inevitable part of life's process. The certainty is that we are all going to die. The uncertainty is in how we live and travel along life's path. People had choices and happy people always looked good in their old age. Olivia was always positive but sometimes it could be hard to be happy. Happiness is like the ocean. It rolls in and out at will and when the tide turns it goes as quickly as it came.

You have to be patient and wait for your ship to come in. As a person grows older, they understand more, they have wisdom, and they are grateful for all the happy moments that come their way. Unless, of course, they are a grumpy, unhappy, negative, old person and Olivia didn't have time to think much about those people.

CHAPTER EIGHT

A few hours later Olivia left the world behind to walk into the wonderland that was Central Park. She was free for the first time since she arrived in this glorious city. She was going to have some well-earned 'me' time. First stop was at the Asia Dog. A typical stand selling hot food that Olivia had seen many times on American films. She wasn't too keen on the specials and really couldn't see how fish sauce would go well with a frankfurter. The hot dog was massive, with lashings of onion and tomato ketchup. It was more like a hot donkey than a hot dog. Why did things have to be so big in America? Everything was so loud and so in your face. How was she going to get such a big sausage in her mouth? She managed, but not without dribbling sauce down her chin. She knew that she would suffer later with indigestion, but not to worry, it was worth it.

Olivia was beginning to miss home and the moors, the peace and quiet that she was so used to. As she began to walk down the path into the greenery and peace of the park, the calmness and serenity that was lost to her in the week returned, tenfold.

Before she left the hotel, Olivia had transferred everything from her suit pocket into her jeans and now, she took the piece of paper, that Marcia gave her earlier out of her pocket. She didn't notice the card that fell out and fluttered to the floor. A voice began to shout after her. "Excuse me, excuse me."

Olivia turned and pointed to herself. "Are you calling me?"

A cockney voice said, "Yes love, this just dropped out of your pocket, might be important."

Olivia took the card and, without looking at it, thrust it back where it came from. "Thank you. Are you from England?" she asked. She looked at the young man before her, he reminded her of someone, but she couldn't think who.

"I am Wayne Stringer, at your service. Care to walk with me or sit a while, perhaps we can chat and I can make you smile?" Olivia laughed and said that, yes, she would love to sit a while.

She loved meeting new people and was always on the lookout for characters for her books. Wayne told Olivia that he was studying at New York University. He liked poetry and was staying with his friend, Sam, up in The Village for a while. He liked to come down to the park for inspiration.

He said, "I am sure I have seen you somewhere before. Let me think." Wayne studied Olivia's face when it came to him. "I know," he grinned. "You are that writer, erm... Olivia Orphanidias?"

"It's Orphanidis," Olivia replied. Wayne grabbed Olivia's hand and began to shake it vigorously.

"You are famous, oh brill," he enthused.

Olivia began to blush. "I wrote a book, that's all, nothing to be famous about."

"Yes," he said. "But what a story, it kept me guessing. I was in a rush to see what happened and you left it open ended. Is there going to be another one to finish it off?"

Olivia wasn't sure how much to tell this cockney boy and went on to say, "Yes there is. I have nearly finished it."

Wayne, in his excitement, went on. "I couldn't put it down and the sex bits were much classier than that other sex book, much more realistic. If Jane Austen had written sex, then you must be her reincarnation."

Olivia laughed. She embarrassed herself writing the sex bits. She was very graphic and left little to the imagination. "That other sex book was received like a contemporary *Lady Chatterley's Lover* and made the lady a lot of money," she said as she smiled at Wayne.

"Did you see the film?" she asked.

"Yes, I did," he said. "No comment! I hope you make yours into one. I can see it as a film. Don't stop writing, Olivia." Wayne sighed and looked at his watch. "It has been lovely talking with you. I'm well made up. But I have to be somewhere now. Can I call you? Perhaps we could have a night out on the town? I think my friends would love to meet you. We go out to blues and jazz clubs on Thursdays if you aren't too busy to come?"

Olivia took one of her cards out of her pocket. "That might be rather nice, Wayne, it's been nice chatting, call me." Wayne kissed Olivia on the cheek and ran off into the crowd.

Olivia sat for a moment stunned. "Yes," she thought. "Maybe I am famous. My, Oh, my!" Olivia looked down at the piece of paper that she was still holding. As she unfolded it, she saw that it was a handwritten colour coded map. She read:

'If you follow this then you won't get lost.'

"Bless you, my friend," she thought as she began to study it.

Olivia could not believe it. Marcia remembered all that Olivia had said about where she wanted to go and what she wanted to see when she came for her walk in the park. Olivia had all afternoon to walk the walk and there were three places that she really wanted to see. It would take more than one afternoon to see everything the park had to offer. She began to follow the map.

Olivia's mind never switched off. Her obsession was music and she began to think of songs with the word 'walk' in them. A song that sprung forward immediately was, 'Walk in my Shoes' by Gladys Knight, a good old Northern Soul classic. The one that got her reminiscing was 'I Walked Away,' by Bobby Paris. She could never forget that song.

A long time ago, a boyfriend dumped her on Facebook by sending her that song. That day she was driving across the moors from Sheffield and stopped to look on the internet. She was surprised to get such a good signal and she took a peek at her Facebook page. It was such a shock to see the song posted by the man who said he loved her. She knew straight away what it meant and cried all the way through Huddersfield. He later said he was sorry for what he did and they continued to see each other for a year after that.

During that time, he came to live with her three times, each time returning back to his wife. The last time she told him not to come back and kicked herself for wasting two years of her life, on a liar. When she first took up with him, he never told her he was married. She found out by accident. It was too late then. She knew how easy it was to fool yourself into thinking you loved someone.

It is easy to settle for second best in desperation. Then the one comes along and you really know what love is and know that before you never loved at all. It was just a word that people said to get what they wanted. Olivia was still hoping that the love she craved would one day find her. People were always looking for love or peace or something else. Did anyone actually ever find what they were looking for? Does a person have to compromise and sometimes settle for less? Olivia's experiences taught her not to settle for less. It would be better to be alone than to not have someone who ticked all the boxes.

Sitting in front of the William Shakespeare statue, which Olivia thought to be awesome, she mulled over some facts. She was full of useless, interesting information. She stored it in case it might come in handy in one of her stories.

The very first film to be shot in Central Park was *Romeo and Juliet* in 1908. Olivia saw Central Park in many films and now she was sitting in it. Over three hundred and five films contained scenes of Central Park. Why couldn't she remember any now? It didn't matter as her mind was wandering in a pile of waffle.

A tall man walked by wearing a bright yellow jacket. He had lots of thick black hair and a moustache that looked like a brush on his top lip. He looked like a throwback from the 'seventies; a Tony Orlando lookalike. Then she remembered a film. The man looked like Borat. The least said the better! Sasha Baron Cohen was a very clever and funny man. He appeared rather controversial at times and knew no boundaries. The film was very funny; rather tongue in cheek. As she smiled to herself, Olivia wondered what a conversation between Borat and the Bard might have been like? No, not Borat but Ali G doing one of his famous interviews might be better.

Shakespeare might have written Borat into *A Midsummers Night's Dream*. He would have fitted in with Pyramus and Thisby as one of the peasants. Shakespeare loved quirky characters and Borat was the quirkiest to come out of the mind of Sacha.

Olivia sat back watching the people walking by. She closed her eyes and found some peace in the mayhem of her thoughts. She stopped the waffle and tuned into the sounds that made the park come to life.

Next stop was the Margarita Delacorte memorial. This was a statue of Alice in Wonderland. The mad hatter, dormouse and white rabbit were all there with Alice sitting on a giant mushroom. Margarita Delacourte was the wife of George Delacourte (a publisher). She would read the story Alice to their children and when she died George donated the bronze sculpture to the children of New York and as a memorial to his wife.

Olivia first saw the statue on the television. The programme was called *Don't Tell the Bride*. The groom got twelve thousand pounds to plan their wedding without consulting the bride. The bride wasn't sure what to make of it all, but she settled into it, and everybody enjoyed themselves.

He wanted an Alice in Wonderland theme and took the unknowing bride to New York. Olivia thought she would love to see the statue one day and now here she was sitting across from it. Olivia's mind began to wander again as she remembered another *Alice*. The musical, that her children's theatre group performed at the Edinburgh fringe festival. It was the same year of her affair with Adam.

She didn't need those memories right now. They came for good reason. She knew not why. Olivia looked across at the statue and gave a big sigh. "Adam, why did you have to be on that plane?" she spoke to herself. Olivia pushed the memories away. She wasn't going to let anything spoil her afternoon out. Olivia got up quickly and walked away, leaving her thoughts by the statue. Her hair was escaping from the pink bobble holding it back, as she walked away from Alice. There was a new determination in her step. A determination not to think about Adam.

Olivia went in search of Strawberry Fields. She was not paying attention to where she was going. She was feeling upset and anxious. Not concentrating, she ended up at edge of the lake. This was not on Marcia's map and not part of her plan. Olivia knew, through her life experiences, that it wasn't always the wisest thing to have a plan.

Plans had a way of going wrong. Many of her gone-wrong plans took Olivia on detours from her life path, and no one could say that they weren't adventures. Olivia had lots of experiences in life, some of which she would rather have missed. The positive was that without all the crap she would not have blossomed into the flower that she now was.

She sat down on the grass and picked a dandelion. Olivia studied the bright yellow petals. She once told a woman that she was the Dandelion of the Rolling Stones song. She quoted some words from the song. The woman was suitably impressed. "So, you knew them?" she asked.

Olivia left the woman wondering by saying, "Sorry, I can't say any more." People could be so gullible sometimes and believed what they wanted. It was their fault if they misconstrued what someone else said. People believe what they want to believe. They see what they want to see and that isn't always the truth.

Time was passing and Olivia really needed to find the John Lennon memorial. She followed her nose and eventually came to the Imagine circle. What a wonderful place. There were lots of people walking about or sitting and chatting noisily; yet there was an underlying feeling of calm. There were flowers placed on the circle that was the centrepiece of the area. Tourists were taking pictures and a solitary young man was playing Beatles songs on a worn-out guitar.

Olivia was fortunate to have entered her formative teenage years listening to the Beatles and other bands that were part of a phenomenal music revolution. There wasn't a Beatles song that she didn't like. Her dad would sing 'Paperback Writer' and 'Ticket to Ride' to her. They were the ones he liked best.

The Beatles wrote over two hundred songs, not just for themselves but for other performers. They dominated the sixties with their simple singalong melodies. Olivia particularly liked the Cilla Black version of 'Love of the Loved' and Esther Phillips singing 'And I Love Him'. The Beatles' love songs were succeeded by story songs. Songs such as 'Eleanor Rigby' and 'She's Leaving Home' struck a chord with Olivia.

The songs painted pictures in her mind of sad women. The words of Lennon and McCartney allowed the imagination to run riot, provoking thoughts that touched the heart.

Olivia looked down at the beautiful mosaic Imagine circle and she said a prayer. She asked for peace in the world, food for the starving and health for the ill. Olivia thought of others a lot and knew just how lucky she was in some areas of her life. She also prayed that she would not go into her elder years alone. She hated being alone. Sometimes a person needed a hug and hugging oneself seemed pointless.

An advocate of peace and music, John Lennon was taken too young and yet, maybe his job on earth was done. Olivia firmly believed that a person died when their job on this earth was finished and that sometimes their job continues after, as their memory lives on. John Lennon lived on in his death, he would never be forgotten.

A melancholy mood accompanied Olivia as she moved away from the camera clicking tourists. She usually took lots of pictures wherever she went and cursed herself that this time she forgot her camera. Perhaps she might visit the park again before she left the city. She could look at other people's videos on You Tube. A person could go round the world without leaving their armchair. Oh, the wonders of technology!

Back in the hotel, feeling low and morose, Olivia opened a bottle of wine. There was always one cooling in the fridge. The staff at the hotel always made sure that her fridge was full of superb nibbles of cream cheese fresh salmon and wine. She sat down and noticed the phone flashing. There were five messages. Olivia already knew who some would be from. Marcia would be reminding her what time she needed to be ready in the morning.

Olivia was to address a reading circle at the New York Public Library. There would be enthusiastic, budding authors wanting to know how she wrote her book and what inspired her. They always asked the same questions. Was it true? Was it all imagination? How many hours a day to write? Did she do it for the love or the money? What did she do when she got writer's block? Olivia never got writers block, she did a lot of thinking and then just wrote and wrote.

The novelty of public speaking was now wearing off. Olivia found the Americans too happy and smiley. They were lovely but their intensity was too much in her face and she sometimes felt trapped. Enthusiasm was well and good but too much of it became cheesy.

She pressed the button on the machine to hear Anne chirping at her. "It's great here in Spain, the garden is looking so beautiful... I really must go for a few runs in the woods. The wine is taking over... How are you...? Shall I come over and be with you...? Are you lonely...? Anyway, I better go as have to get some shopping done and then some serious sun loving... Call me... Love you." Anne always finished her conversations with, 'Love you'. It always made Olivia smile. She was missing Anne but really did not want her to come to America.

This was her adventure and hers alone. She was not sure why, but she knew there was no room for Anne and her blonde moments on this trip. She wondered if she might have some blonde moments of her own.

Olivia went and sat by the window, taking the bottle with her. She spent the rest of the evening looking across the tops of the trees, across Central Park to the other side of the city. She was tired and a little scared. She was not sure what she was scared of. Perhaps she wasn't scared at all, just completely exhausted. Olivia was so alone in this big city. She looked up at the night sky and its twinkling stars.

A large teardrop slowly made its way down her cheek, followed by another, then another. Unidentified tears began to fall into her hands as she cried. She watched a hand puddle form, magnifying the lines that crossed her palms. The lines that told the story of her life, past, present, and future, were fast becoming wet. Olivia wiped her hands on her skirt and picked up the bottle to pour another drink. Oh no! It was empty! She took the empty bottle to the kitchen and, as she made her way to the bedroom, her big sigh was followed by, "Oh well, tomorrow will soon be gone and I shall be one step closer to going home."

When Marcia arrived the next morning, Olivia was up and dressed, on her third cup of coffee accompanied by her third slice of toast. Marcia enquired, "How are you feeling today after your walk in the park?"

"I am feeling good, and ready to meet the world today," Olivia replied.

"I need to ask you who this guy is in Los Angeles?" Marcia asked.

"He got in touch with me before I left home and said he might like to make a film, so I told him that I would fly out and meet with him when I was free," Olivia replied, feeling a bit like a naughty schoolgirl and not knowing why.

"OK, I understand that. What do you know about him? Perhaps I need to check this out for you?" Marcia looked worried.

"No Marcia you don't. You do far too much for me as it is. I can do this one on my own." Olivia went on to tell Marcia that the man whose name she had forgotten would be calling her and they would arrange to meet in a week or two.

"Shall I come with you then?" Marcia wanted an answer.

"I don't know. I don't know anything any more. I am coming to the end of my tether here. I love you to bits, but will you please just slow down a little?"

In the lift down to reception Marcia got her answer. Olivia turned to her and said, "Would you mind if I did this film thing on my own, please? I don't mean to be rude." Olivia looked at Marcia with a determination that said, 'back off'. Marcia backed off even though she felt uneasy about the whole thing.

As they were heading for the front door of the hotel Olivia's name was called. "Excuse me, Miss Orphanidis. Excuse me." The receptionist was waving an envelope at her. "This just came for you by courier," he said.

Olivia took the envelope from him. "Thank you," she called as she walked quickly out of the building.

"Are you going to open it?" Marcia was wondering what it might be. "Could be important," she said. Olivia looked at the envelope which gave no clue as to the contents or where it was from. She opened it to find a plane ticket and a short note.

'Looking forward to seeing you, Olivia and hope we can do business. Shooting just now down at Myrtle Beach so hope you don't mind coming down here?'

It was signed Mal.

"I can't believe this," Olivia said in surprise. "We were just talking about this. It's from that man, Mal. A return ticket to Myrtle Beach," she continued. "I am sure he said he would ring me first?"

Marcia frowned. "Are you sure about this Olivia? I don't feel good about it."

Olivia grinned. "You can't believe how excited I am now. I am going to discuss a film. I am going to Myrtle Beach. It's a place I have wanted to visit for so long and wondered if I could fit a trip in down there. How weird is this? Marcia, all I do at home is listen to Shag City Radio. I am rather obsessed with the music, and I love the way they dance. I can't believe this. Oh, my goodness!" Olivia often said, 'Oh my goodness!' It meant she was happy.

Olivia turned to Marcia. "The ticket says this Friday and I return Monday. Have we anything on?" Marcia told Olivia that they could move things round anyway, as this was important to her and asked that she keep in touch regularly as she was not happy about Olivia flying around America on her own.

Olivia assured her that she would ring every morning and every night while she was away and asked that Marcia meet her at the airport on her return. Later in the day Olivia was checking her wardrobe and beginning to sort out the clothes she would take with her. Nothing too fancy but more classical and casual would be best. She needed to create a good impression if she were to get the film deal.

The flight would be about two and a half hours long and Olivia began to charge her tablet up so she could read the latest book she bought from Amazon. It was 'The Empress of the East' all about how a slave girl became Queen of the Ottoman Empire. Even in those days there were formidable women. Olivia didn't like flying that much and reading helped. It would be good to get out of New York for a while and see some of the country. She fell asleep on the sofa dreaming about her trip to Myrtle Beach and the film that might result from her meeting with Mal.

CHAPTER NINE

As the plane was coming in to land Olivia watched the surf hitting a long stretch of beach. The sunlight was bouncing off the flat lands before her and at last she was going to see Myrtle Beach; that which she had longed for. Olivia hoped to do some dancing while she was in South Carolina and possibly sign a film deal with Mal. She couldn't remember his last name. She had worked so hard to find someone who was interested in turning her book into a film and she was more than excited. It was quite stupid really coming all this way to meet a man called Mal and not knowing anything else about him, apart from that he wanted to make a film of her book. She did not listen to Marcia and her doubts about going it alone. Olivia always thought she knew best. It was hard for her to take advice and she rarely listened to others or her inner self. She would never listen as she felt it was up to the individual to make their mistakes and mistakes are good learning curves.

When Olivia opened the envelope in New York that held the plane ticket she found a note which asked that she take a cab from the airport to her hotel and that someone would pick her up and drive her to the film location. Olivia was now making her way to the arrival's hall. The interior of the hall was a warm beige and full of shops. She did not stop to look in them.

One airport shop is much like another and she was eager to get out to the beach whilst there was still daylight. Olivia pushed her way through the double glass doors to the airport lounge, which wasn't busy at all. She noticed a young man with a shock of red hair, wearing a blue shirt, standing behind a row of balloons. Each balloon had a letter on it. She was intrigued and moved closer to see what the letters were. The young man was holding a bunch of multicoloured flowers.

Above the normal airport noises, she heard a song playing in the background before noticing a tiny stereo player by the young man's feet. She listened a while and recognised the song. It was 'Let's Get Married' by Al Green. Olivia was twenty-two when the song was released. It brought a rush of memories back and she began to smile. She wondered if it was some kind of advertising campaign, as a woman in a black and white sweater was speaking to the man while she fiddled with a camera. Olivia stopped to watch the proceedings. She didn't have to wait long as a young woman came out of the double doors. She was wearing a white T-shirt and ripped denims, her long black hair hanging down her back.

The young man walked across to greet her. Olivia moved closer and just as the young man got down on one knee, she deciphered the letters on the balloons. They spelt, 'Marry Me'. Olivia sighed as she continued to walk out of the airport into the Carolina sunshine. She smiled and felt envious. So romance was not dead after all. She could not remember when someone last did anything romantic for her. She searched the filing cabinet in her brain and found a long-gone memory of when she lived with Charlie.

***

Charlie was younger than Olivia and the relationship lasted ten years. It was Christmas and all she wanted was a big red bin she had seen in the local furniture shop. Christmas morning, she found it under the tree all wrapped up in red and green paper. Charlie seemed awfully excited about the red bin and hovered around her like a humming bird. Olivia kissed him and thanked him for having listened to her. Charlie said it wasn't the only present and she needed to look inside. In the bottom of the bin Olivia found an envelope with two tickets in it.

The next day Charlie and Olivia set off to spend the New Year in Austria. St. Wolfgang am Wolfgangsee was the most beautiful place Olivia had ever seen. It was covered in snow, was so pretty and was a holiday she had almost forgotten.

***

Once outside arrivals Olivia soon found a cab to take her to the Ocean Beach resort. As they drove through the security gate, she was confronted by a massive set of buildings that looked out onto the ocean. Olivia was getting used to the massiveness of America now and was happy to close the door on the world as she entered her bedroom. She quickly unpacked and signed in with Marcia. "The flight was really good, and it is so warm down here. Yes, the room is lovely too, stop worrying, Marcia, I will be fine and back with you before you know it." Marcia told her to make sure that she texted her whenever she went somewhere and not to sign anything without her seeing it first. Olivia appreciated the care but didn't like it at times. It made her feel like a child. That made her into a rebellious child and that could be very dangerous.

That evening Olivia was standing outside the hotel when a pink Cadillac pulled up. It was a very warm day, and she was wearing a pink T-shirt and tight blue cut-off jeans, topping small navy mules. Her long hair was hanging loose and she had a navy rose holding the side back. The late afternoon sunlight caught the white that blended with her blonde. It was a shimmering vision of spun silver. Olivia clutched a small navy bag nervously. She knew that whatever happened tonight it would be an adventure. She could feel it in her bones.

"You Olivia?" asked a dark haired, rather good-looking man. He showed a small diamond in his front tooth as he smiled at her.

"I am," she replied.

"Well hop in, missy. Vic is going to give you the ride of your life," the man said.

"Who is Vic?" she asked, realising that it was a stupid question when it was obvious.

"I am Vic and I am here to serve you for the duration of your stay." He said as he jumped over his side of the car and ran round to open the back door for her.

"Do I have to sit in the back then, Vic?" she asked.

"Well, missy, not if you don't want to. You can sit right up front with me." Vic opened the front door. Olivia sat down and took her sunglasses from her bag.

Well, she might as well look the part. It was something she excelled at: posing. There wasn't much call for it on the moors of Yorkshire which was more of a baggy sweatshirt, jogging bottoms and wellingtons sort of place. Being warm was more important than looking like one of the jet set. She certainly was feeling more like a member of the jet set, doing lots of posing in America and enjoying herself immensely.

Vic began to talk to Olivia as he pulled out into the traffic. Even though she was sitting right next to him she could hardly understand what he was saying and he had a lot to say. Olivia had three things to contend with, the noise of the traffic on one side, the ocean on the other and Vic's accent. Olivia tried to concentrate for as long as she could and hoped he would not ask her a question. She began to realise that Americans had different ways of speaking and the dialects were more pronounced than those in England. It was sometimes difficult as people also had different senses of humour and ways of saying things. Olivia smiled. She suddenly interrupted Vic with the question. "Vic does everybody down here listen to Shag City Radio? I listen to it all the time in England."

Vic turned and looked at her. "Why we sure do, missy. I just love to shag, don't you?" That was it. Olivia could not contain herself and began to laugh. The quizzical look on Vic's face made her realise that she would now have to explain herself.

"Oh Vic, I am sorry I am not laughing at you, it's just that the word 'shag' means something very different where I come from. My friends are always laughing at me when I say shag dancing. I hope to do some while I am here."

"You want to do some shagging while you are here then?" Vic asked.

Olivia giggled. Vic carried on. "You mean shag doesn't mean dance? You don't do shag over there?"

Grinning, Olivia said, "Oh yes we do but In England it means, fuck."

Vic thought about this for a moment and laughed, "Oh I see. I think you and I are going to get along really well, missy. I shall look after you and if there is anything you need you just ask Vic." Vic drove for about forty minutes before turning down a dirt track. Olivia began to panic.

"Vic where are you taking me?" she asked.

Vic replied, "Don't worry yourself none, missy, they all on location in a field. They soon be finished for today."

"Oh," was the reply.

Vic went on to tell Olivia that the film was called *Coming in the Corn*. The title could have meant anything, and Olivia's imagination woke up and began to run riot through her thoughts. She began to imagine aliens landing their space ship in the corn field and decided it was probably a sci-fi or zombie film and would be a blockbuster. Zombie films and sci-fi were very popular. Olivia loved sci-fi but zombie movies were much of a sameness and watching dead people with slobbering bloody jowls eating live people didn't leave much to be desired.

Just as Olivia was going to ask Vic what the film was about, they pulled into a clearing. To the left were two massive trucks and the biggest pink motor home Olivia had ever seen. Somebody obviously liked the colour pink. A group of people were sitting on benches at a long table that was covered in a pink gingham cloth. They all stopped talking and turned to greet Vic. He jumped out of the car and ran round the side to open Olivia's door as he shouted, "Hey guys, meet Olivia." He bowed and swept his arm across the group. "Olivia, meet the crew."

A few smiles and 'his smile' came back at them.

In her best Yorkshire accent, which sounded quite posh next to the southern Carolina drawl, Olivia said, "Hello everybody, I am very pleased to meet you." She chuckled to herself. Now, where on earth did that come from?' She could have just said 'Hi.' A young woman with bright red hair stood up and beckoned to Olivia to come and sit beside her. Olivia sat down and someone poured her a drink.

The redhead said, "This is to welcome you. A local drink." Olivia took the shot that nearly choked her. She spluttered as the heat of the alcohol began to turn her face into a luminous fire.

"Good grief!" she said. "What was that?"

A young man down the table said, "That lady, is Southern Comfort, Peach Schnapps and Chambord mixed with pineapple juice and we call it a South Carolina."

Raising her glass, Olivia grinned. "Would it be rude to ask for another one?" She had a feeling that she was going to get on with these people that were sitting in the cornfields.

Olivia looked round to see Vic talking to a man who was stepping out of the pink motor home. They were deep in conversation. She watched them and assumed that the man was Mal as he looked across at her, smiled and waved. What a strange looking man he was. She could only describe him as a mixture of Barbie's Ken, a seventies medallion man and Freddie Starr. He was like Ken as he had the same hair, thick and blonde almost looking like a wig. Medallion man because his shirt was unbuttoned to the waist, and he was wearing a very large gold chain round his neck. Olivia hated gold chains around a man's neck and never understood why they had to be so big. Historically it was to signify wealth, status and prestige. Rather like a peacock showing its feathers, maybe? Or was it to make up for small stature in man bits?

Mal gave Vic a friendly pat on the back before turning to walk towards Olivia. Olivia found it hard not to laugh as he had the same walk as Freddie Starr and was also quite short. Freddie Starr was a controversial British comedian in the seventies. A person either loved him or they hated him. There wasn't a middle of the road with that man. As Mal walked towards her, stopping now and then to speak to a member of the crew, his actions brought to mind the impersonations that Freddie Starr did of Hitler. Freddie wore trouser cut-offs, wellingtons and was very, very funny. Freddie was also an amazing Elvis impersonator. He wasn't everybody's cup of tea as sometimes his boyish antics got the better of him and he could get out of control, but Olivia loved him.

The smile Olivia was wearing turned into a grin as Mal said, "Olivia, how wonderful that you are here." Olivia rose and stepped over the bench holding out her hand.

"You must be Mal?" she asked.

"Sure am, sweet pea, Mal at your service." Mal did a mini bow and then grabbed Olivia and kissed her on both cheeks. Olivia stepped back and looked at the man standing before her. Mal took hold of Olivia's hand and took her to a small table placed outside his abode. She sat down as he asked, "Can I get you anything?" She was feeling rather overwhelmed by this little man and his gold chain.

"No, I am fine, thank you."

Olivia smiled and Mal smiled back. She began to feel a little uncomfortable. Her instincts were trying to tell her something, but she wasn't sure what. Mal excused himself as his phone rang. "I have to take this, it might be important; it's work, work, work and deadlines. You know how it is." Olivia nodded. No, she didn't know how it was. She was just being polite.

Mal listened to the caller for a moment and then began to speak very loudly. He sounded very annoyed. "What do you mean she won't do it? Of course, she will. Is she still there? Put the bitch on." Mal looked at Olivia and mouthed, "Sorry, won't be long." Returning to his conversation Mal said, "Look Honey, we are paying you a lot of dollars for this... yes, I know... you said you would... you signed the contract... for Christ's sake he's not that ugly. How was I to know he had bad breath? Give him a fucking toothbrush then..." Exasperated, Mal finished with, "You're not the only long-haired, bitch down here you know, some girl would bite my hand off for the part. Look I am in a meeting right now but will see what I can do."

Mal switched the phone off and beckoned one of the crew. "Give the woman what she wants and make sure we don't use her again, I don't care how good she is there will be someone better, we just need to find her, this one's been trouble right from the start."

Returning to Olivia, Mal said, "I don't know, Olivia, these wannabe divas. What is it you say in England? Give them an inch and they take a mile?"

Olivia laughed. "Yes, they do. I don't mean to be rude Mal, but it has been a long day."

"Yes, yes of course," Mal continued. "Sorry, I had to bring you down here. We're behind schedule and it costs money, a lot of money. I hope Vic didn't bore you too much on the way down," he said. "You and I have talked lots on the phone already and you know I loved your book and I think it might do really well. That book of yours is a real winner. If we can sort something out after I have given you my slant on things, we might be able to come to some arrangement that will be beneficial to us both?"

Olivia nodded and said, "I don't see why not but I can't discuss this now Mal, I really am too tired."

Mal could see the weariness in Olivia's face and said, "OK, sweet pea. Tomorrow we are shooting a party down at the beach, perhaps you could be in shot as we film, part of the crowd or something? I know you are going to be famous, and this could be a cameo role. Shoot's not on till four and goes into the night so perhaps we can meet earlier, and I will show you around?"

Mal took Olivia by the hand as he spoke and began to lead her back to the car. Olivia looked across at the crew, who were still drinking and seemed to be having a good time. "I don't see why not, I have done some film extra work before," she replied. "I wouldn't be able to finalise anything about the film until I have spoken to my PA and the publishers. She wasn't best pleased about me coming down here alone, what with it being my first time in America. She worries a bit."

Mal turned to the crew and said his goodbyes. He linked Olivia's arm and pulled her back towards the car. He got into the back with her. All she wanted to do was return to the resort, have a light supper and curl up in bed with her book.

"Where are we going now?" Olivia asked.

"There is a little seafood restaurant down the coast, a way, I thought you might be hungry?" he replied as he opened a box that Vic placed in the back of the car earlier. Mal took out two flutes and a bottle of pink champagne. He held it up and asked, "All right with you?" Olivia nodded. She could see that she would not be going back to an early night anytime soon.

Olivia was tired and was thankful that this man did not have the same dialect as Vic. She did not have to concentrate to understand him. She settled back into her seat and raised her glass before taking a sip. Mal launched into a speech, "Welcome to my world, Olivia. May we have a long and fruitful relationship that will make us both a lot of money. Now tell me about the sequel as we might be able to make one feature instead of two." Olivia shrank back a little, beginning to wonder what she had got herself into. She felt totally out of her depth.

Olivia was a plain Yorkshire girl who never thought anything would get this far. She had only written her book for pleasure and it appeared that she had a real talent with a skill as a storyteller to be developed in future books. Here she was, sitting with a filmmaker in his pink Cadillac driving down Myrtle Beach in South Carolina, drinking pink champagne. She knew she was about to have another adventure and began to miss her friend, Anne.

Olivia wondered if she should have asked her to join her on this trip. They would both have enjoyed their time with Mal and he would certainly have liked Anne. She was more flamboyant than Olivia and was a master in the art of flirting. Mal would have loved her. Maybe she could have been in his film? She would have loved that.

After filling up on the best seafood ever, Olivia once again said to Mal, "I don't mean to be rude but I'm very tired."

"So sorry sweet pea," he said. "I just got so carried away with meeting you and forgot about the time. Of course, we must get you back or there won't be any point in going to bed." Mal paid the bill and soon they were outside Olivia's hotel.

Before they said their goodbyes Mal said he would come up with Vic to the hotel the next day and take her for a tour of Myrtle Beach and then further down the coast where they would be filming. Olivia asked him what the film was about. "Oh, you know, the usual thing. Boy meets girl with a few twists and turns." She was just about to ask Mal if it was a Zombie film or a sci — fi when her head began to pound. That awful feeling when one is overtired ran through her body and she closed her eyes.

She had really had enough of Mal for one night. She could not wait for him to go. A warm bath and hot chocolate were calling to her. If you were to ask Olivia what Mal talked about during the evening, she would not have been able to give a true answer. She thought it was something to do with the film that he was in the process of shooting. Soaking in a hot tub full of bubbles Olivia remembered the drone of his voice and how it went on and on. She closed her eyes and began to listen to the sexy sax of Ronnie Grieco. She was looking forward to the next day and the filming. Being an extra in a zombie film might be quite exciting.

CHAPTER TEN

The following morning after a good night's sleep Olivia was out on the pavement in front of the hotel enjoying the Carolina sunshine. She was dressed casually in a black silk vest, cerise shorts, black diamanté flip-flops topped with a white, wide-brimmed floppy hat. Dark glasses concealed her tired eyes and she looked every bit the film star. Olivia was apprehensive about the day ahead and the butterflies were playing in her tummy. She still wasn't sure if she would take part in the film shoot but thought she would enjoy the beach party. It was time to let her hair down. She had one shot at this experience and she was going to enjoy every minute of it.

Mal and Vic arrived on time and ever the gentleman, Mal got out of the car and kissed Olivia on both cheeks after which he said, "My, you are looking mighty fine this morning young Olivia."

She laughed and said, "not so much of the young Mal, still feeling tired after yesterday. It has been non-stop work since I arrived in America and at times, I think I am looking forward to going home. What have you got planned for today nothing too strenuous I hope?"

"Do you like shopping?" Mal asked.

"Doesn't every woman?" was the reply.

"Well then," he said, "that is what we will do. We will hit the stores. Have a coffee at the Sun City Cafe. My friend Jim owns it and we can get a cake or something if you like. I have some surprises for you so I ain't saying much more." Olivia looked at Vic, who winked and smiled at her.

After a few hours of shopping when Mal would not let her pay for anything, they walked into the Sun City Cafe.

A tall, well built, bald man in a red checked shirt with sleeves rolled up to reveal bulging, over worked biceps, came from behind the counter and greeted them. "Mal, you old coyote, not seen you in here for a long time, where you been?"

Mal replied, "Hey Jim. Yes, I know and I shouldn't neglect my friends. Been doing back-to-back films and if the work's there, I have to take it."

Jim looked across to Olivia and asked, "And who is this pretty little missy?"

Mal looked at Olivia as he said, "This Jim is my English friend, Olivia. She is over for a couple of days."

Jim took her hand and shook it hard. "Nice to meet you, Olivia, you must be important. Mal always keeps his women friends well hidden."

Mal was not her friend. Just because he took her shopping and bought her stuff did not mean they were friends. There are all types of friends, and he was way down the pecking order, more of an acquaintance and not even that really. They were just doing business together. Olivia was just about to set the record straight when Jim walked off behind the counter.

Whilst Mal and Jim carried on chatting Olivia carried her bags down onto the terrace and sat down in the shade. She watched them from her seat. They seemed very intense and she wondered what they might be saying. As they were busy, Olivia took her phone and sent Anne a text:

I bet it's raining in Ilkley and here I am sitting in Myrtle Beach after shopping. I got you some lovely pressies. The man paid for it all, how about that? And am off to a beach party tonight.

It wasn't long before her phone pinged. Maybe Anne sat by her phone waiting to hear from her? Or perhaps she was out on a long walk when she took her phone with her to measure how many steps she'd taken.

As Mal and Jim joined her a message came through. It hadn't taken Anne long to reply.

Bitch! Yes, it's raining. So, have you met him then, the filmmaker? What's he like, tall, dark and American? Why is he buying you stuff? PS. Thanks in advance for my lovely pressies.

Olivia quickly tapped out the reply;

Nooo... more like Freddy Starr's brother. He is buying me stuff because he wants to make an impression. Probably got a very small dick so throws his money about. I am having a laugh though and I think there might be an adventure soon, just a gut feeling. Wish you were here. Love you xx.

Jim took the opportunity to chat to Olivia. "So how long you here for? A few days I hope?"

Olivia didn't think she liked Jim much and the word 'smarmy' came to mind. Why would he want to know how long she was staying? She also got the pleasure of a stale underarm aroma as Jim put the glasses on the table. Olivia could not cope with smelly men. She kept her face straight as she replied, "Just a few days and then it's back to New York."

Olivia wanted Jim to take himself and his smell away. The face behind her mask was showing distaste and a sort of frown that said, 'Fuck off, you don't stand a chance'. Not very ladylike but there was something about Jim that made her feel uncomfortable and brought out the tough Yorkshire lass in her.

Jim carried on, "Mal just invited me down to the beach party tonight, perhaps we could have a drink and chat later? I got to work now."

Olivia, ever the lady, put on her posh Yorkshire voice as she replied, "I might be busy, we'll see." Just as Jim was about to reply he was called away.

Olivia sighed with relief, 'thank goodness, why would I want to chat to him?' she thought. Olivia didn't really want to chat to anyone. She wanted to rest and sign a contract. Maybe party a little and then go home.

Olivia made a mental note to herself that perhaps she needed to dress down a bit in future and she so wished that Anne was with her now.

Nobody noticed Olivia when she was out with her best friend. Anne was gorgeous, had personality and hair to die for. She carried her own limelight with her. It was always switched on. Men hovered round it like moths and Anne loved the attention.

Olivia pushed her chair back as she said, "will you please excuse me I need the lavatory." Mal nodded and began to tap out a number on his phone. Once inside the cafe she looked around until she saw a sign at the back of the room under an archway. When Olivia came out of the cubicle and began to wash her hands, she heard the door go behind her. She saw Jim enter the small washroom. She thought perhaps he was coming in to clean. How wrong she was. Jim narrowed his eyes and looked her up and down. His smile was as creepy as he was.

"Why does Mal get the best? Perhaps it's his power?" He leered at her.

'Oh God,' Olivia thought, "here we go." She didn't know whether to ignore him or engage in the conversation.

Olivia turned back to the mirror and began to apply her lipstick when Jim came up behind her pinning her against the sink. She was powerless and could not turn round as Jim suddenly put his hands on her breasts and squeezed as he said, "These can't be real!"

Olivia knew she needed to take control over the situation and smiled as she said, "Oh but they are." At the same time, she drew her foot up and ran it down the front of Jim's shin. He let go of her and jumped back, startled. "That hurt!" he winged. As he bent down to rub the front of his leg, Olivia poked him in the eye and made her escape.

She quickly returned to the table and said to Mal, who was still on his phone, "Right let's get a move on, time to go." She picked up all her bags and marched out onto the pavement without looking back. A startled Mal finished his call and ran after her.

As he began to catch up with her, he said, "Olivia, slow down, what's the matter?"

Olivia kept on walking and shouted over her shoulder, "It was just time to go. I don't want to be out all day, could we go to lunch now, please?"

An hour later they were enjoying lunch at a local restaurant, The Sea Captain's House, adjacent to the beach. A bottle of sparkling wine resting in the ice bucket complemented the seafood platter that they were sharing. There was enough on the platter to feed six, not two. Mal, for once, was quiet. He couldn't eat and talk at the same time. It was obvious he liked his food as he slobbered over the lobster. Olivia welcomed the calm and looked out at the ocean. For once there were no thoughts in her head, only the sound of the waves and Mal finishing off his lobster. The way she had dealt with Jim made her feel proud. She still had it in her, despite her years. Olivia was enjoying the slight breeze and the sea air and thought she might take a nap when she got back to the hotel before getting ready for the party.

After the desert, as they sipped their coffee Olivia said, "Would you mind if I went back to the hotel, Mal? I am rather tired and would like to rest before tonight."

Mal smiled and tapped her hand. "Aww! That's fine Honey. I need to get down to the location as I don't trust the crew to get it right and we hope to start filming before the sun goes down. How about I get Vic to pick you up? You call him when you are ready. Don't worry about food there will be plenty there. Hog roast, creamed corn and the works. Locals will be coming too There will be a band and you might get to do some shagging. Didn't you tell me that you liked shagging? You can shag with the band. We won't be doing the serious filming until after midnight and most people will have gone by then."

Olivia smiled (that word! Shagging!) what a difference from dancing. She asked Mal what she should wear. Would it be chilly later? Mal told her Myrtle was like most resorts, cooled down at dusk and then began to warm up again into the night. She could come in shorts but bring a sweater or wear whatever she wanted.

Half an hour later Olivia walked into her hotel room, threw her bags down in the corner and lay down on the bed. Before long she fell into a deep, deep sleep. It was a much-needed sleep that would leave her refreshed and ready to party.

Olivia was woken by the phone ringing. For a moment she forgot where she was. She leant over to grab the receiver and missed, falling off the bed, sending the phone crashing to the floor. She swore, something she didn't do often and retrieved the handset. "Hello," she said, "Sorry about that, I fell off the bed." Olivia began to laugh.

Marcia laughed at the other end of the line. "Hi, Olivia. How is it going?"

Olivia sat down on the bed and replied, "It's fine, but they talk in a dialect I can't always understand and some of them seem to be stuck in a time warp." Marcia asked what she meant. "Oh, you know, sort of in the seventies. The way they dress. Their attitude to women."

Marcia laughed again. "So, when are you coming back, please? You are sounding good, and I have a few appointments set up for you. Do you think you might be doing business down there, film wise?"

Olivia sighed, "It might be possible. Everybody is being very nice and looking after me. I had a good day, got some shopping done and had a lovely lunch overlooking the beach. Being picked up in an hour to go to a beach party. It is a scene in the film they are shooting. They were in the cornfields when I first came. Everybody is so friendly. The film is called, *Coming in the Corn*."

Marcia asked, "What is it about?"

Olivia walked over to the bar and poured herself a glass of wine as she continued. "Don't know really. Thought it might be a zombie movie or perhaps sci-fi. I didn't think to ask. I am sure I might find out tonight so I will call you tomorrow when hopefully I have cut a deal." They spoke for another five minutes before Olivia went to run a bath. She was to be picked up by Vic at six thirty.

The drive down to the beach was so relaxing. Olivia felt good and Vic chatted about nothing much as the sun turned into a perfect orange before it began to slowly dip into the turquoise horizon. Vic took Olivia to a trailer parked at the side of the beach. It was pink. He told her that he would be around most of the evening if she needed him. A worried look crossed his face.

"What's wrong Vic?" Olivia asked.

He looked embarrassed and replied, "nothing, missy just tired and you remember what I said?"

"Yes, yes I do," she smiled as he walked away. Olivia felt safe with Vic, more so than she did with the slimy Mal.

She didn't have time to wonder what that was all about as Mal came up beside her. He took her by the arm and into the pink trailer. It was crowded and Mal began to introduce her as author of the year. He left after finding her a place to sit in a corner. Olivia watched as three women were transformed by make-up artists. Wigs, false nails and false eyelashes complemented the glossy lipstick and tanned skin. Olivia was a little confused by their clothing which looked rather raunchy and risqué for a beach party and a film shoot, until she remembered that this was South Carolina and perhaps that is what people wore. This place was a million miles away from the Yorkshire Moors and the culture she was used to.

Olivia chatted with the girls for a while. They were really pleasant and very friendly. The tallest one who obviously had breast implants asked, "Are they your own, Olivia?"

Olivia pointed to her chest. "You mean these? Yes, they are all my own."

The girl replied, "Then you are very lucky to have some like that at your age."

Olivia didn't know how to take that comment or what to say and answered, "Well I suppose it's all down to the foundation garments one wears."

Mal brought a man over to meet Olivia. She could only describe him as a Mr Universe lookalike. He was very tall, and his biceps were like massive molehills stuck to his arms. His name was Bart he had stubble and tattoos that were of Chinese origin. They stood to attention whenever he moved. Olivia found a man with stubble could be rather sexy. Bart did not look rather sexy. He looked as though he needed a shave. Two other men joined them. Equally gym fit, wearing T-shirts that did not really fit them. They were named Al and Bob. Olivia looked up into Al's eyes. They were the most beautiful blue she had ever seen and as she began to get lost in them, he took her hand and said, "Hi Olivia, Mal hasn't stopped talking about you." Olivia felt a tingle all the way up her arm as the memories of her last love hit her heart, the memories of a man who broke her and left her to her misery.

Bob, on the other hand, was not as good looking as Al but he had a presence about him that was rather attractive. They were all waiting for the crew to set up on the beach and Olivia sat back looking at the actors who were getting ready for the party. She felt her instinct move again. There was something she wasn't quite sure about but could not quite put her finger on it. They certainly did not look like zombies or science fiction characters, but perhaps they would change into them as the party progressed?

By the time the sun was hitting the west, the party was in full swing. Olivia was unaware that the cameras were rolling until Vic took her to one side. He said, "you OK about being at this party?"

She laughed. "Yes of course, why wouldn't I be? I love a good party and this one looks good to me." She held her glass up to his face. "This drink is good too, what's this one called then?"

Vic replied, "it's a blue dolphin, has a kick in it that makes you smile."

Olivia spoke as she burped, "Oh yes, of course, and it is... making me smile."

Vic frowned as he asked her the question. "Missy, how many you had? Are you drunk?" His look of concern was not expected.

"Oh Vic, don't be such a stuffed shirt. I'm rather merry that's all. I love a good party and I'm a big girl. Don't worry. I can look after myself." Olivia pushed Vic's shoulder in jest.

Vic continued. "Missy do you know what this is? Do you really know what is happening here?"

She turned to search for another drink as she answered, "yes. Mal explained earlier, it's a beach party and he is going to try to get some good silhouettes as the sun goes down and they might be filming into the early morning; see the sun coming up. Anyway, zombies only come out at night, don't they? Or is that vampires? Listen, Vic, I will be returning to England soon so let's enjoy tonight."

Vic gave her a strange look before he turned and walked away saying to himself, "zombies, vampires?"

As the bonfire blazed and the Carolina Beach Music blared out across the sands the cameras began to roll. Mal danced up to Olivia. He said, "Hey, sweet chic you OK with being in shot?"

Olivia thought for a moment and then slurred back at him, "Hmmm… me thinks best not. But I am enjoying the party and I love the drinks."

As Mal took Olivia by the hand he said, "OK, sweet pea, come with me." He dragged her to the edge of the stage, where the DJs were working their music magic and before leaving her to get on with his work said, "stay here, then you won't get caught on camera. Enjoy!"

A live band began to play as a waiter walked by carrying a tray of drinks. Olivia grabbed two, before sitting down on the sand to watch the party. She would dance later. After the singer stopped talking in a drawl, she could not understand, the group began to play 'I am a Man of Constant Sorrow'. Olivia closed her eyes and remembered one of the funniest films she'd ever seen. It was called *Oh Brother, Where Art Thou?* starring George Clooney. She loved George Clooney and she loved him more when she heard him sing. This singer didn't sound like George Clooney, but he gave a good rendition. The song was originally written in 1913 by a blind Kentucky fiddler named Dick Burnett.

Lost in the words of the song Olivia didn't notice the man standing before her until she opened her eyes. She was looking at two gigantic feet in front of her. They were brown and big. These feet were very unhealthy looking and perhaps could have done with a wash. Olivia slowly looked up to see a man wearing ripped denim shorts and a grey T-shirt with the words, 'It's all real' emblazoned across the front.

"Now then," he said, looking down at her with a leary look on his face. "You look all alone so perhaps I should sit awhile." He didn't wait for a reply and promptly sat down beside her. He was far from sober but that didn't matter as she wasn't either. "You one of the actresses then?" he asked.

"No," she replied. "I am visiting from England."

He wasn't listening to her and went on. "You look mighty fine to me, are you one of the girls in the film?"
Olivia laughed, having made up her mind earlier that this was a zombie film, she could not now imagine herself to be looking like something dead. She did wonder if perhaps she'd been heavy handed with her make-up and that perhaps made her look frightening.

"So, you do films across the ocean?" he asked. Olivia began to think he was a complete moron and again thought this man could be in one of her books, perhaps she ought to show some interest.

"What's your name and what do you do?" she asked. He told her his name was Daz, and he was a hog farmer and had been working out a lot by lifting his hogs. The hogs didn't seem to mind but one day one threw up all over him and one bit him, so he thought he best invest in some weights or go to the gym. Olivia tried not to laugh. Daz said he hoped to have a main part in Mal's next film and perhaps he might use him tonight in this scene.

Olivia, who was more than drunk now, said, "You don't look like a zombie to me." Daz looked at her as though she was totally mental. Maybe she was. He had never met an English woman before.

"What the fuck she on about?" he said to no one in particular, "Mal said nothing about zombies." In his tiny farmer's mind Daz did not believe Olivia when she told him she was a writer. She just looked like a blonde with big tits who was in the film. They began to chat about the stupid things two drunks chat about and were getting on rather well. Daz was beginning to like Olivia. He went to get two more drinks. The group finished their set, and the DJs came back to play some tunes that Olivia loved. This was becoming one of the best parties she had ever been to. Her obsession was music and they were playing some good old northern soul tunes. When Daz returned Olivia was leaning against the stage under one of the giant speakers that was blasting out, Sandy Barber's, 'The best is yet to come'. Daz danced towards her and winked. He was thinking, 'Oh yes, little lady, the best is yet to come!'

Olivia thanked Daz and was wondering how she could get rid of this hog farmer. She asked him about his hogs, and he was in his element telling her all the names he had for them and how they needed special attention. She wasn't sure what 'special attention' meant and thought it was best not to ask. No woman had ever paid him such attention before and Daz was beginning to get the wrong end of the stick. He began to think that Olivia more than liked him and without warning Daz lunged at Olivia and grabbed her round the waist. He pulled her to him and before she could retaliate, he silenced her with his squidgy lips and stuck his tongue down her throat. It was obvious that he was looking for her tonsils.

Totally repulsed by his beery, hog breath and the male hardness that was now sticking into her leg, Olivia slowly moved her hand which made Daz loosen his grip. Oh yes, Daz was going to enjoy himself with this little English missy. Taking advantage of the moment Olivia quickly put her hands between his legs and grabbed his testicles before giving a swift turn of her hand which nearly broke them off. Daz jumped back in horror clutching his masculinity as tears crowded his eyes.

Olivia, losing the last of her decorum, shouted, "Fuck off you awful cretin, how dare you?" Daz felt a hand on his shoulder as he was turned round and punched by an irate Vic. The hog farmer fell to the ground and Vic stepped over him. He took Olivia by the shoulders, "You OK, missy?"

Olivia could not believe what had just happened. "I'm fine Vic, could I have another drink please?" she asked.

"Don't you think you have had enough? Shall I take you home?" he said.

Olivia slowly looked up at Vic, with a look he had come to know and he soon returned with a drink in hand. She had now composed herself. The incident having sobered her up somewhat. "Thanks Vic," she said before running off to join the dancers, shouting back at Vic as she went, "let's get the party started, it's time to shag. Yippee!" Olivia still could not get used to the word shag meaning dance. Vic watched as she disappeared into the crowd.

A few hours later Olivia was fast asleep in a sand dune by the ocean. She slept the sleep of a drunk. She woke after only a few hours and sat up in the darkness wondering where she was. Looking in the distance towards the ocean she saw the burning bonfire and remembered. That was some party! It was quiet now and there didn't seem to be many people around. She peered through the darkness and she saw people standing at the other side of the bonfire. She slowly got up and walked towards the camera crew. She still felt drunk from too many blue dolphins, which was probably a good thing as the hangover from hell was hovering around waiting to pounce.

As Olivia neared the fire, she felt its warmth. She began to wonder where all the others were and whether the cameras were still rolling. Where had all the people gone and why was it so quiet? Olivia saw Mal and Vic standing close together. What were they looking at? She crept up behind them and peeped over their shoulders. They did not know she was there. She was about to get the shock of her life as she side, stepped and said, "Hello boys."

Then she saw them in front of her. Olivia saw Bart, Al and Bob with the tall girl she had spoken to earlier in the day. Her hand shot up to her mouth and her eyes widened as she saw a scene from years gone by. It brought back memories of Felix and Hamburg. The night when she threw caution to the wind and her nightdress flew across the room before she pounced on the man from the airline.

It brought instant feelings of her time travelling round Germany with the Into the Sun people. Just then Bart turned into the spotlight.

"Oh my God!" Olivia gasped. Surely that wasn't his penis? No way could that have been anyone's penis? It was massive, quite the biggest sausage she had ever seen. It was huge, purple and erect. As Bart moved Olivia saw more. The blonde was up on all fours with Al's erection in her mouth and Bob was busy thrusting and groaning into her leaking vagina as he pushed backwards and forwards. What on earth was this? They didn't look like zombies. They were not making a zombie film, not a sci-fi either. As Olivia turned away in absolute horror, her eyes met Vic's. Then she knew! They were the last thing she saw before she fainted.

The breeze and smell of wafting underpants brought Olivia round. One of the crew was bent over waving a pair of black and white underpants over her face. She didn't know whether to laugh or cry. Olivia could see Mal and Vic looking down at her. Concern was written all over their faces. Mal began to twitter, "you OK, sweet pea?" he asked.

Vic added, "you gave us such a fright, I don't think you should have drunk so much, missy."

Mal looked at Vic asking, "do you think we should call the medics?"

Vic shook his head. "No, I think I need to take her back to the hotel. It's been a long day for her. We don't want her to get sick now, do we?"

Olivia closed her eyes, the image of the last thing she saw before she fell ran into her vision. The blonde… they were… massive unreal purple rod… Bart was a donkey! As she sat up, she felt the vomit as it rushed out of her mouth and sprayed all over Mal's shoes and his legs. Would this mean that they were not friends now? Mal began to scream as the contents of Olivia's stomach hit him, no longer the cool medallion man but more the idiot wimp. He turned and ran into the ocean, arms flaying and screaming, "Oh no, my Gucci's, my Gucci's!"

Vic helped Olivia up off the floor, his arm supporting her they walked slowly back to the car. "Come on Missy, I think it's time you went home." The silence in the car was deafening. Olivia felt ill. She was tired and very confused. What had she gotten herself into? Vic drove slowly as he did not want a repeat performance of Olivia and her discomfort.

She turned to look at him. "I am so sorry, none of this was meant to happen."

Vic laughed. "It was all worth it to see the look on Mal's face. He was always going on about those shoes, drove me crazy. It's going to keep me smiling for a while to come."

Olivia began to search in her bag until she found her phone. She sent one text before they reached the hotel. It said:

You are never ever going to believe this. Never in a million years. Zombies, Vampires and Aliens, Ha-Ha!! How could I have got it so wrong?

Pressing 'send', the message flew oceans away to Yorkshire and her friend Anne.

The next morning, just as Olivia opened her eyes, a hammer with the word 'hangover' written on the handle began to pound in her head. As the fog of her drunken sleep cleared Olivia began to wonder, how long had she slept? How did she get home? She wished she could remember. What happened? She turned to look at her watch which told her it was already lunchtime.

She turned over to go back to sleep when her phone began to burst her ear drums. She reached across and took it from the bedside table and saw she already had four missed calls. Olivia pushed the button for loudspeaker and whispered, "hello." She sounded like a dying frog. "Hello," she said once again. A familiar voice made her smile. It was Anne.

"OMG!!" Anne said. "What has happened? You sent me that text and then didn't pick up the phone. I nearly got on a plane and came over."

'Oh no,' thought Olivia. 'Please don't do that.'

Olivia began to speak slowly and told Anne the story of her encounters, firstly with Jim and then with the hog farmer. She heard Anne laughing. Olivia protested, "it's not funny, it is not funny at all. They were a pair of 'plonkers'." She began to remember more and Anne laughed more and more. Eventually Olivia joined her and began to laugh. Looking at things the day after a drunken binge brought things into perspective. "And then when I sat up and puked all over his Gucci's and he ran screaming into the ocean! Well, you can imagine."

Olivia continued to tell Anne of the day and the porn film. Anne spoke, "Has Mal been in touch then?"

Olivia wasn't listening, "I really don't know, I don't know what to make of it. I really don't. It is my own fault, no one made me drink, but those blue dolphins were to die for. I just couldn't stop. I was back in my teenage days and just went a bit batty."

"What will you do now?" Anne asked.

Olivia thought for a moment and replied, "No idea, haven't a clue." She was stopped by a knock on her door. She said her goodbyes to Anne and slowly walked across the room, her head continuing to pound. Vic was just about to knock again when Olivia opened the door. He could not get over how beautiful she looked, even though it was obvious that she was the worse for wear.

"Come in," she invited. She walked back across the fluffy beige carpet feeling at least double her age.

Vic said, "Sit down, missy. I will get you some coffee." They sat together sipping the hot espresso and Vic began to talk. He asked her what she wanted to do. He told her that Mal wanted to see her and he had gotten over his sea trip, although his shoes were now ruined.

"Oh my, do you think I should buy him some more?" Olivia said. "I think I am dying."

Vic said, "I can see that, so here is the plan. You shower and I will sort some food out." As she was about to protest Vic jumped up and took her by the arm and led her to the bathroom door. He gently pushed her through it and said, "You don't need to buy Mal any shoes, he got plenty. Make yourself human now. Food be here when you resurface."

Half an hour later they were sitting on the balcony, enjoying an early lunch of fries, bacon and eggs, followed by pancakes. Olivia made a mental note, 'Salads when I return home!' Olivia wasn't quite sure what to say to Vic and felt rather embarrassed by the proceedings, the night before.

They discussed what happened. "Vic," she said, "I had no idea that it was a sex film, no idea at all."

"How so?" he asked. "I told you the title."

"Yes," she said. "Coming in the corn. I thought it was a zombie film or aliens."

Vic laughed. "Olivia, how do you think they spelling the word?" He spelt the words out for her. "It is c-u-m-ing not c-o-m-ing."

Olivia felt the heat rising to her cheeks. "Well, I just assumed," she said.

"But Olivia you know that someone reviewed your book and said it had more class than that other sex book. Did it not occur to you then that someone might want to make a porn film out of it, especially after that time in Hamburg with that man, Felix? I read your book; it was really good!"

Olivia finished the last of her pancake before saying, "I have been a little naïve really, haven't I?" Vic smiled and nodded. "I think I need to go back to New York, Vic. No point in hanging round here. There was more to *Chasing Rainbows* than just sex."

Vic nodded, "I know. It was a psychology of relationships and really showed the differences between men and women. I loved that you wrote it from a male perspective too." Olivia looked embarrassed once again. Vic told her he would check the flights to New York and get back to her. He had to report back to Mal. He said Mal couldn't understand why she had been so upset and wanted to come to see her. Olivia said she couldn't cope with that and just wanted to leave.

Vic gave her a big hug, walked towards the door and turning he said, "You know, missy, it has been a pleasure driving you around. That Yorkshire charm has bowled me over and I won't forget my time with the missy who has the biggest smile and the loudest voice to warm the coldest heart."

As Vic closed the door, a giant tear ran down Olivia's face, she was going to miss Vic and she suddenly felt so lonely. She sat down like a little girl lost. She was always alone when all she wanted was a significant other to love her. Her whole life she searched and searched for that one true love. She thought back to the last man. He was awesome. He was everything she had ever wished for. Her Mr D'Arcy was a dream come true. It lasted six months and they were the best she ever had in her whole life. She loved him so, but he didn't love her so and he also decided to stay in his situation. He never lied to her about being married but she lied to herself and that was stupid.

When his email ended it, Olivia did not cry, she could not cry. Her heart wasn't broken as he had taken it with him. Two years had passed and she still lived in hope of his return. Yes, she was certainly stupid, and she was certainly crying now. She put her head against the chair arm and the sobs escaped.

Olivia thought she would never stop crying. She wrung her hands in the anguish of one who had lost the love of her life. She fell into an exhausted sleep and dreamt that she was sitting by the ocean. She dreamt of a man she couldn't quite see. He walked towards her and, as he came nearer, he faded into thin air. Disappeared just like all the men in her life. They had their way with her, used her and walked away. It wasn't long before Olivia was winging her way back to New York.

CHAPTER ELEVEN

"I can't carry on. I can't do this. It is all getting ridiculous. It has got to stop." Olivia was pacing the floor in front of Marcia, who was sitting on the sofa before her. Olivia was extremely agitated, rubbing her hands together and jumbo tears were washing her face. "How stupid have I been? I should never have gone down there. I should have listened to you Marcia. I am a product of my own imagination." Olivia was totally exhausted, both physically and mentally. She had just flown in from Myrtle Beach and couldn't stop crying.

A very concerned Marcia patted the space beside her. "Please sit down, Olivia, tell me what happened? Was it so bad?"

Olivia stopped and stared at her. "Bad?" she whimpered. "No, I wouldn't say it was bad. Bad is not a good enough word to describe it. In fact, I think for once in my life I am speechless." Olivia thought for a moment. "It was unacceptable, yes lousy and unacceptable!"

Marcia smiled. "That bad? Shopping was that bad?"

"Oh Marcia," Olivia sat down next to her on the sofa. "Well, maybe not that bad. I did meet some nice people and a few twerps. How could I have been so stupid? Sometimes, my arrogance gets the better of me and my worst enemy is my own enthusiasm. My whole life I have never stopped to think, just jumped in with my boots on, so to speak."

Marcia rose and went to pour them both a glass of wine. "You know, Olivia, it pays to research and talk to others, and I did say but you weren't listening."

"Bring the bottle," shouted Olivia. "There is dire need for alcoholic conversation, me thinks." Olivia smiled to herself and shook her head. What a fool she was. When would she ever learn? Marcia brought two glasses and a bottle of Pinot Noir, Olivia's favourite. Olivia dried her tears, and they drank in silence. Marcia was thinking what to do for the best. It was obvious that Olivia was cracking up; heading for the edge of the cliff and that would not do, as she had many commitments booked in the next few weeks.

Marcia had to weigh up where her loyalties lay, with Olivia or with her employers. She reckoned both. Her employers wanted her to look after Olivia and that was what she was trying to do. She had grown very close to this loveable Yorkshire woman in the few weeks they had been together. She loved the Olivia, who most of the time kept things simple. What you saw was what you got. There were no hidden agendas. Not like some of the people she had to look after. Olivia was laid-back and just got on with things. She had a wicked sense of humour and there wasn't a day that went by without them both laughing. Even when Olivia called her from Myrtle Beach, the way she recalled what happened had them both in stitches, which made Marcia wonder why Olivia was so upset now. She felt that Olivia was just overtired.

Olivia jumped up and began pacing the floor again. "Olivia please, sit down, please," Marcia said. She was very worried. Olivia was going into meltdown. Meltdown causes breakdown. Breakdown causes havoc and then everything might stop for a very long time. "Olivia, what you might need is a pill." Marcia smiled. She had some in her bag. HTP5s were herbal remedies and helped Marcia when she was down. Before the HTP5 Marcia used to take kava. They were brilliant but, as they had been found to cause liver cancer in six people out of the thousands that took it, the herb was taken off the market.

Marcia bought some kava off the Internet. It came all the way from Hawaii in an old, battered tin. Next time Marcia felt she was losing the plot she took some. After about an hour her face began to twitch. She threw the rest in the bin. Marcia's friend, Juniper, told her about HTP5. Juniper figured she was a healer using meditation and herbs, Marcia loved her but knew she was an airhead and would have been happier in the sixties and seventies. It wasn't as good as the kava, but it did the job.

"No," snapped Olivia. "I do not need a pill. I don't know what I need. I know what I do not need. No more book signing, no more interviews, no more middle-aged women with sexual problems."

Olivia found that her book had awakened women to their sexual needs and their problems. They took it as gospel that the words in Olivia's story were what a man should be doing to a woman. Women would creep up to her when she was at a venue and ask for a private word. Women might get sexier as they get older, but a lot of older men (husbands) just got problems and Olivia thought if she heard another moan about erectile dysfunction or premature ejaculation she would turn into a melancholy madam. Perhaps what they said to her would go into her next book. What did she know about sex with men? She could draw on her own experiences from her past, but it had been such a long time since she had her clothes off and laid with a man. One night in a bar in Keighley a man asked her what her sexual preferences were. She was taken aback but thought about it and answered him, "How the hell do I know when I haven't seen a willy in years! Now fuck off you pervert!"

The run up to sex was something she yearned for but really couldn't be bothered with. The 'what is your favourite this and that' and all the stupid things men say to get a woman into bed. What Olivia wanted was love, companionship and loyalty. A tall order at her age as most men were, either married, been on their own too long or wanted a younger model. Some men of her age and older had prostrate problems. They had totally lost their libido. They thought it might return by watching porn. It was all rather sad really. Men her age were creeping slowly to their maker, and she wanted a life. She was healthy enough and wanted to live out the rest of her life being loved like never before. She didn't care about the sex, that would be a bonus. She lied to herself, of course, the sex was important. She just wanted to be part of an 'us' and a 'we'

"None of this is worth losing my sanity, Marcia, not even the money. I think I need to stop right now. I am off for a long soak and hope you will stay and wait for me. We have more talking to do." Olivia hugged Marcia and left the room. Marcia knew that she had to do something for this woman she had grown to love in such a short space of time. She felt for her. Olivia was one of the nicest women she had ever looked after, and Marcia had looked after some class A bitches. It hurt her to see Olivia in crisis. Marcia finished off her wine and went to the window to watch the world go by. The trip down to South Carolina put a dent into Olivia's ego and she had run away from a bad situation. She was not about to tell Olivia that Mal had rung the office several times and couldn't understand why Olivia did a runner. He understood after Marcia had finished with him and he stopped ringing. Olivia had her hopes dashed and Marcia might be able to work some magic here, but she had to think it out.

She began to hatch a plan which would be to everyone's advantage. She left the window and picked the phone up. The phone call was to change everything and keep everybody happy. Marcia was good at her job. She was one of the best.

CHAPTER TWELVE

A few days later Marcia was driving towards the Coast. "I think it's somewhere down here. It's so long since I came up here," she said as she turned the car towards the Ocean. They headed down a pretty avenue and saw a landscape of gold, white and blue. Olivia looked out of the window at the incoming surf. The sun was beginning to set and throwing a dark pink hue over everything. It was a mystical scene and touched the spirit. She hadn't seen anything so beautiful in a long time.

"Look Marcia! We are where we ought to be, in the pink," Olivia laughed.

They drove a few miles along the beach front when Marcia suddenly said, "Look there he is. He is waiting for us." She began to toot the horn and they pulled up outside a quaint wooden beach cottage. Sitting on the veranda was a handsome man wearing white shorts and a black polo shirt. He stood up and smiled. He waved at them as they got out of the car.

Looking around Olivia felt instantly at peace. She was good at getting a feel for places and she felt this one in her soul. Was this heaven? Walter walked towards Olivia and clasped her in a big, all enveloping bear hug. He was an ex-boxer, and she was soon lost in his arms. "Well," Walter said, "You are here at last! It is so nice to meet you after all these years." Olivia once more realised what a small world it was when Marcia told her about her cousin Walter and Cape May.

Olivia and Walter were Facebook friends. Had been for years, ever since he paid her a compliment on the app, 'Who thinks of you'. They had chatted on and off. Walter put wonderful pictures online of Cape May and Olivia never thought she would ever be in that picture. Now she was. She always promised him that one day, if her book was a success, she would look him up. It wasn't just a coincidence, it was synchronicity, more of a meaningful coincidence.

Olivia began to babble, "I am so grateful that you invited me. What a small world it is. Couldn't believe it when Marcia told me you were cousins." Olivia felt safe as she stood in front of this man. She felt safer than she had in years.

Walter began, "We are indeed, our mothers are sisters. We don't see enough of each other." He smiled at Marcia before continuing. "This cousin of mine is too busy in the big world of people. I believe she is staying over with my mom tonight and leaving early?"

Walter looked quizzically at Marcia who looked guilty as she nodded. "When are you going to settle down Marcia, find a nice man and come up here and have a family?"

Marcia, looked at the sky, took a moment and replied, "Never. When are you going to settle down and have a family, Walter?" They both laughed.

Walter continued, "Marcia explained your situation without too much detail. What has been happening is your business. It is the end of the season now and not many people about. Best place to recharge your batteries, rest up and just have some chill out time."

Marcia went to get Olivia's case from the car as Walter led Olivia up to a veranda of the cutest house she had ever seen. The veranda ran right round the building, and they mounted some rickety steps facing the ocean. On a small table by a swing chair there was a silver bucket of ice, housing a large bottle of champagne. He poured some into beautiful crystal flutes, that looked very old and expensive. "These are beautiful glasses Walter. Too good to drink out of."

"They been in my family for years, came over from Ireland with my father's father. I don't believe in keeping things in cupboards, might as well use them." Marcia returned after placing Olivia's cases in her bedroom and they toasted the good weather and wished each other good health.

Olivia began to speak, "I just couldn't take any more, Walter. Myrtle Beach was such a fiasco and I have had enough. I always thought it would be good to be famous, but I'm not so sure now. I am very tired, and I need some rest. I need to give my head a good wobble and spend some time with myself. I am forgetting who I am."

Walter smiled. "I know that one. It happened to me, and I had to give up boxing before it killed me. You stay as long as you need to. No one will disturb you and there is no one else here." He pointed to the other houses dotted along the beach. "I am busy closing them down for the winter. I have one more visitor booked in for next week. Arrives the day before you leave so you shouldn't be disturbed."

They all sat in silence watching the ocean come nearer and nearer as the tide came in. Walter refilled their glasses as he asked, "So what do you intend to do whilst you are here?

"Nothing much," Olivia replied. "I shall do some walking, beach combing, drawing, but mostly resting and soul searching. I need to sort some things out in my mind."

Walter stood up to leave as he said, "Well if you want peace you have come to the right place at the right time. If you need anything, I left my number by the phone. You are invited to our end of season party on Saturday if you fancy coming along as my guest?"

Olivia told him that would be very nice, and she would look forward to it. Walter walked down the steps of the veranda with Marcia as he told Olivia he would call by in a couple of days to make sure she was settling in. The freezer was full and there was plenty of drink in the cupboard. Marcia turned and ran back to Olivia. She put her arms round her and said, "Best place for you right now. Sleep, rest up and by the time I come back for you I will have a meeting set up for you in Philadelphia about the film. Don't start writing another book, just chill. I am at the end of the phone too, that is if you can get a signal."

Olivia spent the rest of the evening on the veranda. She watched the sun go down, the moon come up and the stars begin to shine. She drank what was left of the champagne before exploring the house. She was exhausted and soon climbed into a giant welcoming bed. It wasn't long before she fell into a heavy, dreamless sleep.

During the night Olivia woke once. Very disorientated and not knowing where she was, she walked out on to the beach. The waves crashed in front of her, and she looked up into the night sky to see the lights of a plane cruise slowly through the darkness. A sudden flash back of her flight from Manchester rushed into her mind to haunt her. Adam was winking at her from his seat on the plane. Felix was on his knees pleading with her to forgive him. Shaking her head, she ran back to the house. A cup of tea later, Olivia was snuggled under the duvet and quickly falling asleep again.

The screaming gulls entered Olivia's unconscious and woke her in the morning as the warm sun streamed through the windows of the pretty bedroom. White furniture sat on a stained, highly polished wood floor. Girly frills and pink roses adorned the bed and complemented the sage walls. Olivia felt she could stay in that room forever. She opened the French windows that led onto a small balcony that held a small bistro table and one chair. She sat down and looked out at the bright beach and thought it best to be out there in the sunshine. So, she pulled on a pair of white shorts and a cropped pink vest and scraped her hair back into a ponytail. After a glass of fresh orange juice, she set off up the beach, running towards the sun.

Thus, began a morning routine which provided the best therapy in the world. Exercise and being at one with nature, was all that Olivia needed. In a few days she began to look like a true beach babe. Her skin was turning an awesome gold and her hair was bleaching to a streaky white. Slowly the turmoil that she brought with her was abating. It was being replaced by an inner peace that touched her soul. Olivia was alone and she was happy. She was finding herself. She was learning who she was and what her needs were. She also knew that she could not work out fully where she was going until she looked at where she had come from.

When Olivia first arrived in Cape May, whilst unpacking her bags, a card fell out of one of her pockets. She picked it up off the floor and turned it over seeing it was the card given to her by Adam at the airport, the card that she almost lost in Central Park, which was retrieved by Wayne Stringer, the cockney chap. She was surprised to see that there was also a small inset picture of Adam next to his details. She laughed. He couldn't help himself, could he? He was forever the poser. She too liked to pose. They were well matched. She sat now on the veranda. Olivia always had the radio on, she was obsessed with music and a song began to play. As she looked into the eyes of Adam on the card, she heard Phillip Goodhand Tait singing 'Oceans Away'. It was as if he was singing only to her and a road behind her began to unravel.

Olivia began to solve a mystery that she had carried for long enough. She acknowledged that she was a major player in her past and could have changed things. She had choices. The problem she always had was that she never thought. She jumped into life's opportunities without ever thinking of the consequence of her actions. She thought she knew best. It was her life, and she would do what she wanted. She didn't feel guilty about her past actions. She felt shame. In those shameful times she was out of control. Surely that was someone else who did all the things that hurt her. It was! It was a younger Olivia and now she was older but was she wiser? She hoped she was.

The young Olivia never gave a damn. She ploughed through life with her happy demeanour and mad thoughts. She never quite grew up. As Olivia thought back over the bad times and the good times, she began a slow metamorphosis. She realised that to chase rainbows was futile. She had chased them long enough and now she was oceans away from her past. As the song on the radio ended Olivia could not stop the words of the song going round and round in her head.

> Don't worry now cos you're not dreaming.
> I'll love you always where ever you'll be.
> Oceans away go where you may.

She was oceans away from home, oceans away from her past and she was still dreaming. She really had to stop now. She spent her life searching for something she needed to believe in. Olivia knew it was out there somewhere, the love that she craved. Sometimes she was a mass of contradictions. She believed in love and then she didn't believe in love and many times she questioned if it really existed.

Olivia looked at the card in her hand and with a big sigh dropped it on the table in front of her. She looked out across the beach as she wondered what to do. Then she knew. She picked up Adam's card and after making herself a coffee, she walked to the water's edge. The tide was on its way out. Olivia walked up the beach to a small jetty where some boats were moored. She ran to the edge and threw Adam and his card into the water. Slowly it went further and further out to sea. "Goodbye Adam," she said. "I couldn't ring you now even if I wanted to." As Olivia walked slowly back the way she came, a tear ran down her warm cheek. It was time to move on. Adam should never have been on that plane. He should never have given her that card. They should never have seen each other again in life. Now it was over, well and truly over and Olivia could move on.

A few hours later Olivia was sunbathing on the white beach after a good swim in the ocean. It was the perfect first day in paradise and she allowed her mind to wander back to her conversation with Walter the previous night. The gentle breeze that was leaving the sea to cool her was relaxing to the point of lethargy. She could have stayed by the Atlantic Ocean forever. She could hide from the world. But there was no hiding from the past and the future was yet to come. Sitting up she saw she was alone. The beach was totally empty, and the sun warmed her as she looked out at the glistening water with a few gulls bobbing about on the horizon.

One thought entered her mind and that led to another until she was on a thought wave. Olivia wondered if she was becoming bitter and twisted when it came to relationships and men. There was a certain cynicism making a tracing in her thought patterns and she did not feel comfortable as they brought a tinge of negativity which was alien to her. She began to pull the memories of past hurts from her mind's filing cabinet. The hurts that nearly destroyed her but also made her stronger.

Olivia knew that in order to have someone in your life you had to trust them. But first and foremost, you had to trust yourself. Each time that she was let down, was knocked off her bike, she would get up dust herself down and ride on. Olivia knew she would keep pedalling until she found the one for her. If she passed him by and missed the opportunity for true love then it wasn't meant to be. A gull cried as it flew overhead, taking Olivia away from destructive thoughts that were quickly spiralling down into an abyss of depression.

She lay back on the warm sand and watched the sun disappear behind a grey cloud. The clouds began to shift from her memory and a time gone by surfaced in total clarity. She allowed her mind to take her back into the past to a time she had long forgotten.

CHAPTER THIRTEEN

It was Olivia's thirteenth birthday, and she was back in her mother's village in Santorini. Dino was her first love. He was a year older than her and had a certain attraction about him that Olivia could not resist. At fourteen he seemed such a man. This was a time of innocence when the buds of adolescence were awakening, and the little girl was leaving her dolls behind and recognising her changing body and all the feelings that came with it.

Dino wanted much more than to hold hands with her. They kissed a lot, and he was the first boy to put his hand down her knickers. He was a fumbler and could never quite find her forbidden cave. Olivia would find the whole thing boring, and it wasn't long before she would push his hand away and say it was time for her to go home. The hand in the knickers became almost ritualistic as they played a game of, 'yes, I will, no you won't'. Dino and Olivia became an item that summer and Olivia was sad to leave to go back home to school. She wrote Dino a few letters and, after no reply, she promptly forgot about the boy in the village.

Two years later when Olivia was fifteen, she met George. She was happy. Then, when she was seventeen, she went back to the village in Santorini. Dino came back on the scene and Olivia melted into his arms. Olivia told Dino all about George. He was not listening, and the summer was spent in passionate clinches. They were older now and things went further. The kissing became intense as Olivia allowed Dino to do more to her than before. They continued to play the game of 'no you won't, yes I will'.

Olivia allowed Dino to touch her breasts and the hand down the knickers went further now as she opened her legs to his probing fingers. She never allowed it to go further, and she never took her knickers off, much to Dino's frustration. Olivia had a wonderful summer as the longing of womanhood was awakened within. She resisted the advances of the amorous Dino and returned to England intact.

Olivia went on to marry George and did not return to the village for another six years. This time she was not alone as she brought her husband to visit her family. One night, there was a family gathering.

It was very hot, and the wine was flowing. Trestle tables were lined up in the garden, bending under the weight of the food. Olivia was in the kitchen talking to her cousin when there was a tap on her shoulder and she heard the words, "Look who's here then." Swinging round, she turned to look into the deep, dark, smouldering eyes of a smiling Dino. Olivia began to smile back when George walked into the room and saw them. She introduced the two men and they shook hands.

Dino looked surprised when Olivia told him this was her husband and he made a hasty retreat. She was rather startled by the look she saw on Dino's face at the news that she was married. It was shock mixed with a sort of panic. She began to wonder if all these years Dino had feelings for her and was not just wanting to get into her knickers. George looked at Olivia and said, "I thought you said he was ugly. He doesn't look ugly to me."

Surprised by George's comment Olivia replied, "Well he's no oil painting, is he?" There was an atmosphere between them which soon abated as they returned to the garden to listen to the music supplied by the village band.

Olivia forgot all about Dino until George said, "He fancies you. He has been looking at you all night." Dino and Olivia were sitting at opposite ends of the table. Olivia looked up and her eyes met the dark pools of lust staring back at her. Their eyes locked and the gaze of a moment seemed like forever. Before Olivia looked away, she saw it. She saw the love and the loss in Dino's eyes. Sitting back into her chair Olivia began to wonder if she should have told Dino she was going to marry. She had taken away Dino's opportunity to declare his feelings. For a minute Olivia wondered if she had made a mistake.

At midnight there were not many people left at the party. Those who were, continued to drink, George included. By this time, he was very drunk and would probably collapse into bed without even noticing her. In her foolishness, Olivia got on a bike and cycled across the village to Dino's house. He was waiting for her.

"I knew you would come," he said as he took her into his arms and a passion was rekindled.

"Dino, I must get back," Olivia said.

"Wait I must ask you something," he replied. "Why did you marry without telling me, Olivia?"

She did not know what to say. There was no answer, and it was all too late. She slumped back into the sofa they were sitting on. She felt such guilt. Olivia had not been fair to Dino and now she was sort of cheating on George. Dino and Olivia had not played their usual game of 'yes I will, no you won't'. That was out of the question now. It did not stop their tongues dancing in unison and the most intimate swapping of spit ever.

Just as Olivia was, once more, beginning to wonder if she had made a mistake in marrying George, without warning Dino stood up and pulled Olivia off the sofa, he pushed her up against the wall and kissed her. His hand went down to find the mound he always believed would have been his one day. Olivia stopped him as he said, "Well you aren't a virgin now, are you? Let's make a baby, Olivia and you can tell him it's his."

That was all it took to sober Olivia up and bring her to her senses. This foreign man had no feelings for her. He just wanted to get into her knickers. He wanted to own her punani. Nothing had changed, nothing at all. Olivia pushed Dino away and ran down the path to her bike. She pedalled faster than ever to get back home. She felt even guiltier than she did before.

She should not have left George. He could not speak the language and if she was lucky, he would now be snoring in one of her aunt's chairs. She hoped that she might sneak in without anyone noticing her. This was not to be. Olivia turned the corner and nearly fell off her bike as she saw a very irate aunt standing out in the street. "You don't have to tell me where you have been, madam. I know. How could you? How could you leave this English man here with us? He is drunk and crying for his wife who has obviously become a whore."

The words were like a slap across Olivia's face. They stung and Olivia's eyes began to smart. She was very close to her aunt and never wanted to upset her. Just like she always did, Olivia never gave a thought for others and how they might feel. Shame and guilt showered over her like a wet day in winter.

Olivia thought it would be best if they left and returned to the place they were staying. She found George sitting in floods of tears, very drunk and very upset. "Where have you been?" he screamed at her.

She calmly replied, "I needed some air and went for a ride on the bike."

George got up and lunged at her still screaming, "You have been with him. I know you have. I saw the way you looked at each other. I am not that stupid."

'No, you are not,' thought Olivia. 'But you are that drunk.'

They quickly said their goodbyes to the family and began to walk back to the hotel. On the way back George hit Olivia very hard across her head, twice. Back in their bedroom he gave Olivia a beating she would never forget. She lied to him, and George knew it. She paid for her big mistake.

Ten years passed before Olivia returned to her mother's village with her children. Olivia's aunt had a flat on top of her garage now. She stayed there all summer. Her aunt was happy to see Olivia settled at last. She loved her like a daughter. One Saturday night Olivia went to the local hotel with her cousins. They had a meal and settled down to watch a local singer. It wasn't long before her cousin said, "Look who just walked in. Wasn't he your boyfriend once before?" Olivia turned to look to the back of the room and saw Dino. He was with a young blonde woman. Dino caught Olivia's eye. He waved and smiled. Panic set in and Olivia turned quickly away.

Her cousin, Anna, bent her head and conspiratorially whispered, "That is his wife. He didn't get married for years. I think he was waiting for you to come back."

Olivia laughed. "Don't be so ridiculous. We were childhood sweethearts and nothing more." Olivia took a drink and dared not let her eyes leave the singer on stage. She felt anxious and wanted to leave but couldn't think of a good reason. The night of her beating came flooding back to her. She would not be an idiot again.

Olivia asked her cousin if she wouldn't mind accompanying her to the toilet as she wasn't sure where it was. They excused themselves and left the hall. Olivia kept her eyes in front. She was still reeling from that wave and smile. Everybody would have seen it and it was out of order. A married man did not wave at a married woman, not in that village.

Olivia washed her hands and splashed her face with cold water as she admonished herself. Composed and ready to return to the hall, where she knew the villagers were watching her, she stepped out into the corridor. Her cousin was behind her.

Without warning Dino stepped out of the shadows, in front of her. Olivia jumped. They shook hands and Dino asked, "How are you? I have been waiting for you." Olivia tried to pull her hand away, but Dino was not letting go. Olivia could not speak. No words came and she began to shake. If anyone saw them now, it wouldn't do. It just wouldn't do! Dino leant in close and whispered, "I must see you. I need to see you."

The curt reply from Olivia was, "No."

"Please," he begged her. "I could see you in the park on Sunday afternoon." Olivia was still trying to take her hand out of his. Her cousin Anna watched as their hands went back and forth as Dino kept hold. It became a sort of hand dance and Olivia was becoming annoyed.

"What part of 'No' do you not understand?" she asked. "We are both married now. Behave yourself!"

Dino looked desperate. "Please, Olivia, bring your children too." Olivia gave one big tug and Dino released his grip. She fell over and hit the floor. Dino tried to help her up, but she turned to her cousin for help

"Come on Anna we need to get back, the others will wonder where we are." Olivia glanced at Dino as she swept by. He looked lost and forlorn. She did not care. There was nothing left in her feelings for him.

Olivia blamed him for her beating. He was dead to her. Anna asked, "What was all that about? I couldn't hear what he said. He wouldn't let go of your hand."

Olivia shook her head as she said, "He was just saying Hello. Let's leave it at that." Anna wasn't convinced but she let the matter drop.

The following Sunday in one of her mad, impulsive moments Olivia told her aunt that she was going to take the children to the park. She went to meet Dino. The children played on the swings and Olivia and Dino walked around the green, catching up on the past ten years. The one thing she kept to herself was the beating. It wasn't long before it became clear that Dino was still interested in getting into Olivia's knickers. He still wanted her punani. "Come to dinner on Wednesday," he said. "You can meet my wife, Maria. She will be pleased to meet one of my old friends." Olivia thought that might be a good idea. If she made friends with Dino's wife, he might leave her alone and stop pestering her.

Olivia was very surprised when the following day Dino turned up at her aunt's house and asked if Olivia might be allowed to come to dinner and meet his wife. The aunt said, "Why, yes of course she may come. You have been friends for many years. How nice of you to ask. You are both married now so no harm can be done." How wrong she was!

Wednesday came and Olivia dressed with care. She wore a high-necked dress that came down below her knees and she looked very much like someone's mummy. It would be good to meet Maria and see Dino happy and then she might put the guilt down that she carried for years about not telling him she was marrying George.

Maria was very chatty and presented a lovely meal. Olivia was rather nervous throughout the evening and did not take heed of the amount she was drinking. Dino wasn't very nice to his wife. He snapped at her and ordered her about whilst giving all his attention to Olivia. As the evening progressed, Olivia relaxed a little until she felt a foot under the table. It was slowly creeping up the front of her shin towards her thigh. A hand joined the foot on her leg and Olivia gulped. She began to cough and continued to tell Maria about life in England. There was nothing she could do until she made her escape to the bathroom. Re-entering the room, Olivia realised that perhaps she was a little drunk. This did not stop her drinking more and she made sure that she positioned herself away from Dino's sneaky foot.

By the time it came for her to leave she could hardly stand up. She had done it again, and she was drunk by accident. She was desperate to escape from the ludicrous situation she found herself in and did not really want to be there. Dino was very clever asking her aunt's permission. He knew what he was doing. It sealed the deal and Olivia could not have gotten out of it. "I can walk home, thank you," Olivia said as she stumbled towards the door.

She heard Maria say, "You better take her. It is rather dark out there and not all the street lights are working."

"No Maria I am fine," Olivia said as she fell over the cat.

Dino took hold of her. "I will run you home. There is no way you can walk back in your condition. I would never forgive myself if something happened to you." He put up his hand as Olivia opened her mouth to speak. "No, the matter is settled. I shall drive you back." She nodded. She was too drunk to argue.

CHAPTER FOURTEEN

The next morning Olivia woke with the biggest hangover ever and could not see properly. It was difficult remembering how she even got home. She went down into the kitchen. A black coffee was badly needed. After a very large espresso and a few moans, the fog began to lift. There were lots of questions running round her head with no answers. She was about to return upstairs to the flat when she heard a voice. "Good morning, is she up yet?"

Oh no,' she thought. 'Not now.'

Olivia decided to stay very still, in the hope no one saw her in the little kitchen attached to the garage. She prayed that her aunt might say she was still asleep. Five minutes passed and Olivia decided she would be able to sneak upstairs. She crept out of the kitchen and was halfway up the stairs which ran up the outside of the building when she heard Dino's voice behind her. "There you are!" he laughed.

Olivia was not up for a conversation with Dino, she just wanted to crawl back into bed and die for the day. Dino said, "As you were just coming down, I assume you need coffee." It was a statement and not a question. He went into the kitchen and put a pan on the stove. Olivia could not tell him she was on her way back to bed and returned to her place by the small tatty, plastic topped table that had seen better days. Neither was she going to let Dino know that she was in a most tender state. She really didn't need him there right now.

She thanked Dino for a good night out and the lovely meal. "I think you have a lovely wife. It was nice to meet her."

Dino replied, "Thank you Maria liked you too. She said you must come round again before you go home."

Her first thought was, 'Not likely!' Olivia wasn't really listening now as she was wondering what happened the night before and how she got home.

Dino said, "Well I am glad I drove you back, even though you wanted to walk. I would not have slept for worry."

'So,' Olivia thought, 'He brought me home. I didn't walk.'

Without thinking she said, "Can I ask you something Dino?"

"Why yes of course," he replied.

Two voices in Olivia's head began to argue. One said, 'Just do it. The other screamed 'No, no.' Olivia looked at Dino and she knew she had to ask him. "Err, err, did anything happen last night, Dino? I vaguely remember being in the back of your car?" Olivia watched his face as the question left her.

Dino began to smile. His smile turned into a massive grin. As he reached into his pocket he said, "How could you possibly forget what we did? You insult me. I have waited a long time for you, and you don't even remember!" He drew his hand out of his pocket and lifted a pair of lacy blue knickers high into the air. There was the evidence that he had realised his dream of many years. "Are not these yours then?" he asked. He dropped them on the table and Olivia stared in disbelief. There was nothing to say.

She thought, 'Well it can't have been that big or that good if I can't even remember.' She stared into space and just couldn't look at him.

Dino did not look happy as he rose to leave. Olivia was dumbfounded and felt a wave of shame sweep over her. Since the age of thirteen she had pushed Dino away. She would never have slept with him. She would never have allowed him to have her and yet he did. When she was most vulnerable and lost in drink, he took her in the back of his car without her consent. Or maybe it was with her consent. That would remain forever a mystery. She really must stop drinking. It was obviously not the best thing for her to do.

Olivia didn't know whether to laugh or cry. Her resilience kicked in and she began to laugh. So, after all these years, he did it and she couldn't even remember it. Olivia spent the rest of the day hiding from the world.

She could not undo what was done and it was best to move on from her little foible.

Thus, the affair began. Dino would climb over the gate and enter the flat at night. Olivia resigned herself to the inevitability of it all and thrived in the excitement of doing something she really should not have been doing. She was quite lonely and looked forward to Dino's visits. She didn't look forward to the sex. The sex was rubbish. It was a total disappointment. Dino was not well endowed, and it was sometimes hard for Olivia not to laugh as Dino thought he was some sort of sex god.

Once when they had sex (it could not have been called making love) on a grass verge beside a quiet road, the condom Dino was wearing disappeared. Where it went was a mystery. They searched in the grass for it to no avail. Olivia though it must have fallen off, what with him being so small. The condom was not there. Olivia found it later when she was in the bath. She laughed and laughed. That was a first; a condom left inside.

The time came for Olivia to return home. After many an "I love you. We were meant to be together," from Dino, Olivia boarded the plane and flew home. She spent that autumn waiting by the phone. She expected Dino to call. She expected him to say he left his wife and he needed her to return. The call never came. Olivia was left all alone with the shame of what she did that summer. It was nothing to be proud of. At times there was one good memory which would run into her mind. It was one of when she was closest to Dino. The night when they were holding each other under the stars and the radio played 'How Deep is Your Love' as Olivia translated the words of the Bee Gees. They were close for a moment; bodies locked in their nakedness

Memories are to treasure until they turn sour, and Olivia had a lot to deal with and come to terms with that autumn. She was a cheat and had betrayed her husband. She was not to know that, at the time, he was cheating on her too. That bit of information came out years later. They were both as bad as each other.

The following year Olivia couldn't wait to get back to the village. She wanted to continue where she left off with Dino. There was something exciting about living on the edge. It made her feel vibrant and alive. Being naughty made the adrenalin rush and wasn't that good for a person? It wasn't long before Dino was visiting Olivia's bed on a regular basis once more and they had many perfect moments that would never come again. Olivia was settling into Santorini life and looking forward to the rest of the summer when, one day, Dino came to her looking rather serious.

They were sipping coffee on the veranda when Dino said, "Olivia, I have something serious to tell you." Olivia's heart missed a beat as she knew what he was going to say. He was going to say that he wanted to be with her. They should leave their partners and be together. Dino began. "Something terrible has happened and I believe only you can help me. Not as a lover but as a friend."

Olivia asked, "What?" She was still not sure what Dino was going to ask her, but she remained hopeful. Dino went on to tell Olivia that one night whilst driving on the mainland, he knocked a man over in the road. The man died. Dino was due in court and, if he could not pay a fine, he would surely go to prison, and she would not see him again. He said he knew her husband George had money and she could get it from him if she had none of her own.

Olivia was stunned by the revelation. This was something she had not expected and told Dino that she did not have the amount of money he was asking for and it was very inappropriate that she should ask her husband for it. Downright wicked! Was she wicked enough? She told Dino that she would think about his request and how she might get hold of the money he asked for. Dino told Olivia he needed the money by the sixteenth of the month when he was due in court.

The request ruined the rest of their evening. The atmosphere between them changed and Dino left earlier than usual. It was a very disappointing evening. There was no closeness, no kissing and no sex. Dino climbed over the gate and didn't even turn and wave as he walked down the street.

Olivia was shocked and very confused. Surely this could not be happening. She had always been rash and impulsive when it came to her actions. The request gnawed at her gut and, for the first time in her life, she listened to her instincts. Something was not right, not right at all. She had no one to talk to. If she mentioned this to her aunt then all would be lost. Her secret would no longer be a secret and Dino's visits would have to stop.

Her aunt had never mentioned Olivia's behaviour from the previous year, even though she knew what was going on. She would hear the gate rattle every time Dino jumped over it at night and she said nothing. Olivia's aunt knew her niece to be wild so thought it would be a misuse of time speaking to her and she was not one for wasting her words. The day came when Olivia brought her aunt a drink and said, "I need to talk to you. It is very serious and I do not know where to begin, but talk I must."

Her aunt told Olivia that she could tell her anything she wanted and if she could help her in any way then she would. Firstly, she apologised to her aunt before telling her that she was seeing Dino. Her aunt replied, "I knew you were seeing him. I wondered down the years whether you should have been together."

That remark surprised Olivia and she knew she could trust her aunt. Olivia went on to tell her about Dino's predicament. Her aunt listened. "So that is it," she said. "Well, I really don't know what to say."

Olivia replied, "I don't know what to think. It has all come as a bit of a shock to be honest. Does uncle know I have seen Dino?"

Her aunt frowned, "Of course he does. He is not best pleased with you. You are no longer a child. You are a mother and a wife. Not sure if you are an adult but what you do is your business. We aren't happy that you have used the flat."

Olivia went a deep shade of crimson and began to feel very silly. This was getting out of hand and shame quickly followed the guilt that was rising within. A few days later, a moment arose when Olivia was alone with her uncle. "May I speak with you, uncle?" she asked. Her uncle listened as Olivia slowly told him the story. Uncle rose from the table and brought a small decanter and two shot glasses. He filled the glasses and handed one to Olivia indicating that she should down it. They drank together. The hot burning liquid hit the back of Olivia's throat with a vengeance and she coughed. She sat silently waiting for her uncle to speak. He was studying the bottom of his glass.

After what seemed an age Olivia's uncle looked across the table at her and began, "So it seems you have got yourself into a bit of a mess with this Dino. Do you not think that if he had killed a man in the road, he would be in prison by now? There are no fines for killing a man. It is as simple as that!" The silence that followed was deafening. This was a time when silence was not golden. Olivia asked him what she should do. The reply came. "I cannot tell you what to do. It is your money and your choice. I will tell you to be careful. He is lying to you. That is all I will say on this matter."

Olivia did not see Dino for more than a week. She waited every night for him, but he did not come. Just as she came to terms that she might not see him again, Dino arrived one evening. He seemed preoccupied and in a rush. "Well did you manage to get me the money?" he asked. His tone was sharp and cold. Until that moment Olivia still had not made her mind up what to do but now, she knew.

She said, "I have no money of my own and I have not spoken to my husband. I have spoken to my uncle, and I am sorry, but I shall not be giving you any money. If you have killed someone in your car then, you must pay for it, not me."

Dino looked aghast. He had been confident that he would get the money from Olivia. He did not expect that reply. "Well," he said. "That's it, you won't be seeing me again. Bye." With that he turned and ran down the steps and jumped over the gate.

That was it, the end. Olivia went for a bottle of red wine and sat on her veranda, drinking slowly and gazing at the moon. At this moment it was best to have an empty head. Olivia was so shocked and was not in the frame of mind to process what had just happened. She was hurt and a loneliness began to eat at her heart. This seemed like the worst day of her life. What had she done?

Why had Dino gone so cold? Had he just been after her money. She began to cry when she thought of him in prison. She almost regretted not helping him. Olivia's loyalties were all over the place. She didn't feel good about herself at all. She finished the bottle and fell into a sleep of torment.

Dreams disturbed her as she saw dead men in roads and prison bars. She slept long into the morning and the next day when she woke, she felt her life was over after she lost the love of Dino. The childhood love that had eventually ripened and blossomed was no more. Perhaps he never loved her at all. Perhaps he only loved the money he thought she had.

Two days later, whilst having a coffee with her aunt, Olivia began to tell what happened the night Dino called. When she finished speaking her aunt shook her head and said, "I am so sorry sweetie. You did the right thing, and I really don't think you should be beating yourself up about it like this. You have brought shame on this family, Olivia, with your behaviour. I suppose you have redeemed yourself a little by sending Dino on his way. I suggest you stay in the flat until it is time to return to England." Olivia isolated herself from the family, only going down to the main house for her meals. She kept herself occupied and could not wait for her departure date to arrive.

One morning her aunt knocked on the door. "May I come in?" she asked. She held Olivia's hand as she said, "I know you are hurting, my dear. I love you but I am now going to hurt you some more. There is something you need to know. I wasn't going to, but I can't watch you eating away at yourself because you did not give that man money and you think that you love him" Olivia took a sip of her coffee as her aunt went on. "I saw Dino the other day walking through the village, hand in hand with his wife. They looked very happy. He has not gone anywhere. He certainly is not in prison. I have found some other things out and I ask you to be strong."

Olivia sat without moving and waited. Her aunt continued, "Last year after you left here, Dino had a new roof put on his house. He told people you had paid him to have sex with you. That money paid for his new roof. He also gave his friends intimate details of your times together. This year, Dino and his wife hatched a plot to try and get money out of you. I am so sorry."

Olivia rose from the table. She went to the cupboard and took out a bottle of home brew with two shot glasses. Pouring one shot for her aunt, she took one shot and poured herself a second. Olivia did not speak. She gave a half smile and left the room. She had two more weeks to go before her flight. She beat herself up verbally. She called herself all the nasty names she could think of. How could she have been so foolish? What an idiot! She wondered how many other people would know what happened.

Olivia was full of remorse and shame. She was also very angry and said to herself, 'this is not over you bastard. I will see you again, if not in this life, then the next. Be afraid Dino, I have not finished.' Olivia decided that when she returned home, she would make it up to George. She would be the model wife. What she found when she arrived back in England was that George had not been innocent and he was leaving her for a woman he met when he went to spend some time with his friend. The bottom fell out of Olivia's world twice that summer. She did not return to Santorini for twenty years. She had grown somewhat as a person by then and revenge was no longer on her agenda.

CHAPTER FIFTEEN

Lost in the corridors of her mind Olivia heard a voice calling her, "Olivia, Olivia, are you all right?" She was brought back to the present by Walter bending over her with a look of concern. The distraught look on Olivia's face and the tear trickling down her cheek concerned him and he sat down beside her on the sand. Walter put his arm around her, and she rested her head on his shoulder before her floodgates opened.

The shame, the anguish and the pain of her past ran barefoot across her soul. The tears washed away the years from all her scars and lay bare the wounds that were infected with the word, 'Why?' She turned and looked at her friend. "Why do I end up crying? All I ever wanted was for someone to love me. You know, Walter, I have done some pretty stupid things in my life but never out of malice. I never meant to hurt anybody and just ended up hurting myself. Walter, am I keeping you from something?"

"No, you are good. Just talk if you need to. That's what friends are for." Walter thought how easy it would be to love this woman, but he didn't think it was appropriate to make a move on her when she was obviously in a vulnerable place. He also knew that taking their relationship one step further could ruin the friendship.

Olivia sighed and began to tell Walter all about the terrible times in her past. "Olivia, it sounds as though you have had it really hard."

"I have to acknowledge that I have had a sad and chaotic life and done some things that I am not proud of. Having said that, I have laughed my way through it and I don't cry often." She went on to tell Walter about the journey from Manchester and how she had to confront her past, her long gone past that was on the plane. How she was now terribly confused about her feelings for Adam and was troubled by them.

"It's a small world Olivia and it's rather amazing how sometimes people pop up in the most unusual circumstances. I am not surprised that you are crying, you have been on the go for weeks now, Marcia told me about your jaunt to Myrtle Beach." They sat together for a long while watching the surf as the moon began to sail across the sky. Walter tightened his arm around her, and she lay resting her head on his knees. It wasn't long before she was fast asleep. Walter had proved to be a good friend and confidant. He never asked questions. He just listened. Walter was a good man. Olivia slept while he gently stroked her hair. As the sun began to rise in the east Olivia stirred.

"Walter, have we been here all night? She asked. He nodded. She somehow felt different and thanked Walter for listening the night before and sitting with her through the night as the stars danced on their merry way.

Olivia's time with Walter seemed to have cleansed her spirit. She was ready to go back to her life and move on. "It is good to learn from experiences but not good to beat yourself up about things you have done," said Walter. "If you can't change it then bin it."

Olivia thought his words of wisdom were brilliant but saying and doing were two different things altogether. When she returned to her bedroom she lay on the bed and found a song on YouTube, 'This too Shall Pass' by India Arie. It was the catalyst to release all her negativity and after she ran out of tears, she found herself smiling.

The day came for the end of season party. Olivia was in two minds whether to go or not, but she decided that perhaps after a week on her own some company and new faces might be the thing she now needed. Dressed casually in denim jeans and a large white shirt with her hair hanging loose and gold earrings dangling from her ears, she walked up the main street. She passed Delia's soda fountain and when she got to the end of the street, she realised that she was lost and asked two young men, who were obviously on their way somewhere, if they could direct her to the Harbour View restaurant. They looked at each other before the taller one, who was rather good looking and looked like a typical surfer asked,

"Are you Walter's friend?" Olivia nodded. "Then you come with us, we are going there now."

It wasn't long before she was sitting over the sunken ship which was the foundation of the restaurant. Tod, the young surfer, was busy telling the history of the ship to Olivia as they drank gin and sin, which was served in a large jug. Olivia could not say no to gin and listened to the gorgeous young man with tipsy interest. "The ship was originally called the Utica and when it went out of service it eventually ended up in Wildwood as a gift shop but began to submerge. I think it was about 1968. It was moved from Wildwood to the harbour at Cape May to act as a breaker until 1994 when the owner of the marina, Captain Fred, sank it and built the restaurant over it. How about that?"

Tod and Olivia chatted well into the night. She only saw Walter once as he was busy with out-of-towners who he hoped were going to book his houses for the coming season, the following year. As the DJs began to play, Olivia jumped up and lost herself in the beat. She loved to dance and she left Tod talking to a young girl more appropriately his age. She was happy and at about three a.m. when the party was in full swing, she decided to go home. She left the merrymakers and walked back down the silent main street until she reached the beach.

The following morning Olivia reflected back over her week in Cape May. She realised that she made some good friends at the end of season party and was definitely hoping to return to see them the next time she was in America. Now she was packing her case as she would be leaving early the next day. The few purchases she made in town were lined up on her bed.

Olivia could not go anywhere without some retail therapy. She bought a beautiful cream silk top with embroidered leaves and flowers in autumn colours. Her best purchase was a print. The frame was made of small pieces of driftwood and beautifully scripted words ran across blue waves on pink paper. The words said:

By the ocean I sit with my dreams,
Life does as it pleases, does as it means.

Find yourself as the waves lap the shore,
Love and peace for you once more.

Olivia thought these words would help her in her weak moments and she was now ready to leave all her past behind in Cape May. She resolved to be strong. No more searching for Mr Right. She was happy with herself. She really did not need a man in her life to complicate her chosen path.

CHAPTER SIXTEEN

As it was Olivia's last night on the beach, she decided to light a bonfire, open some champagne and have a party with her new self. She smiled when she remembered the last beach party she attended. Myrtle Beach certainly had some surprises and was a giant learning curve for her. She learnt that perhaps she should sometimes listen to others and that she was not always right. She learnt it is always best to look back with a smile as, without the chaos, the wisdom would not arrive. Her week on the beach taught her that regrets are a waste of time and serve no purpose. Guilt and regrets are the baggage that people carry around with them, weighs them down and stops them living life to the full and she was no longer going to carry any rubbish at all.

Olivia prepared to go down to the bonfire she made earlier that afternoon. As dusk was falling, she noticed the lights were on in the house next door. She wondered who might be there, so late in the season, just as the weather was about to turn. She picked the picnic basket up and forgot about next door. She would be gone in the morning, so it really didn't matter who was next to her.

Olivia lit her fire and poured herself a glass of bubbly. This trip showed her how alone she really was and that it was fine to be alone. If you love yourself and take heed then you can never really be lonely. This new-found independence did not stop her from still craving for that significant other, but she now knew things come in their own good time. If the man of her dreams did come along then that would be fine and if he didn't that would be fine also. Olivia had come far in seven short days, that had gone far too quickly.

She took off her thick woollen sweater as the fire began to warm her. It was lavender in colour and suited her much better than the pinks that crowded her wardrobe. In the creeping dusk her jumper took on fifty shades of lavender and appeared to move on the warm sand. Olivia was slowly replacing the pinks and bright colours with lavender, pale blue and navy. There comes a time in a woman's life that she needs to take a long hard look at the clothes and the colours she wears, and changes have to be made. The new colours were classic and much more befitting her age.

Olivia stripped down to her bikini and ran into the ocean. She felt the cold surf lash against her body as she leapt into the waves. An instant feeling of liberation swept over her, and as she swam around, she laughed; gave thanks for her life and the decisions she'd recently made. As she walked back up the beach Olivia noticed the lights in the house were no more. Perhaps the person was out now. She sighed as she wanted her last night to be totally alone and not with some unknown neighbour sitting next door. The evening was warmer than average and Olivia lay back on her big blue, fluffy towel. She felt at peace.

Dried and dressed, Olivia turned on her small portable radio. She poured another glass of champagne. The radio began to play 'Tango in the Night' by Fleetwood Mac. Olivia just had to get up and move to the music. She couldn't help herself and began to sway to the beat. It was a sensuous dance, and she became totally immersed in the moment. She was alone and she was celebrating. She realised that the bottle by her side was nearly empty. "Oh no!" she thought. "I wasn't going to drink so much ever again." It did not matter. It was the last day of her old life and tomorrow she would embrace her new one.

Lost in her euphoria Olivia floated in another world of feeling wonderful. She was so far away in her relaxed state of dance that she was startled back to the beach when she heard a cough and a man's voice behind her say, "May I join you? It is such a beautiful night and I wondered if you might like some company?"

The voice stirred something in her soul as Olivia stared out to sea. No, she did not want any company. However, her mother brought her up to be polite and she heard herself say, "Yes that might be quite nice." She didn't turn around but moved a few steps backward and sat down on the blanket. She wasn't too happy about her euphoria being interrupted by a stranger. Olivia was about to pour herself another drink when she realised that the bottle was empty. She turned her gaze into the fire that was burning brightly and threw some more logs on to it. She wondered whether to go back to the house and get another bottle. She began to feel awkward and did not know why, as the man sat down slightly behind her. The silence was unbearable.

They sat for a while not speaking until Olivia's curiosity got the better of her and she turned her head slowly to take a sneaky look at her neighbour. She could see that he was quite tall and had good taste in clothes. He was wearing a pair of expensive looking denim cut offs, frayed at the bottom. His striped navy and pale blue polo shirt made a tasteful accompaniment. As the dusk was now falling, she could not see his face clearly. There was a large bottle of unopened champagne by his side. He had his knees up and his arms were clasped round them. Sensing that he was being watched he turned quickly to meet Olivia's stare.

Olivia felt the butterflies in her stomach awaken and begin to do back flips and bounce off each other as she looked into the brown eyes she knew so well. Adam and Olivia gazed at each other and then both smiled. Olivia was speechless and thought she might faint but instead she drank what was left in her glass. Olivia held the bottle up and rather stupidly said, "Well that's it. All gone!"

Adam laughed and replied, "It is OK. I came prepared." He held up his bottle and shook it about. Adam opened the bottle and poured two drinks before handing a glass to Olivia who began to panic. A little voice in her head was screaming at her butterflies to stop.

'Oh my God!' she thought. 'Has he followed me here?' Rationality began to speak to her, 'Don't be so silly. How would he have known you were here?' This was not a coincidence. It was more of a synchronicity experience. Olivia thought about Adam more than once in the past seven days. She had wiped her thoughts clean and rid herself of him and now here he was on the beach with her.

They both began to speak together and laughed. Adam said, "You first."

Olivia said, "No, you first." She felt she could be all right with him and did not feel the same panic she had at the airport many weeks before. A lot had happened since then. Adam moved to sit beside her and placed his hand on the inside of her thigh. It was something he did all the time when they had their affair, especially when she was driving them to the River Ouse. It was a touch of comfort and belonging that she always loved.

"Well," Adam began. "I have not been able to get you out of my mind since I saw you on the plane; after all these years. You are the last person I ever expected to see again."

"Ditto."

Olivia asked herself why she had said ditto. That was really stupid. They sat in silence, each with their own thoughts. Olivia began to feel uncomfortable. She did not know what to say. She did not know what to do. The little radio played in the background. Without warning Adam whispered, "I am so sorry, so very sorry."

Olivia turned and put her finger to her lips, saying, "Don't. Please don't. That was then and this is now. Do not spoil the moment, please." Olivia took a drink from her glass. She had to keep control over this situation and said, "If you start with sorry and raking over old coals all you are doing is moving your guilt to me. You know what you did. You dumped me for my friend. Put the crap down Adam. It serves no purpose, no purpose, whatsoever. Many years have passed, and you hurt me beyond a 'sorry'."

Adam took a drink and looked into those brown eyes he had missed all those years. He said, "I don't know what to say. I don't know what to do."

"Neither do I, Adam, neither do I," she said. Olivia suddenly leant towards Adam and her lips brushed his. She surprised herself. The new Olivia was obviously sleeping as the spontaneity was part of her old self. What on earth was she doing? Olivia was not thinking straight as all she felt were butterflies doing somersaults within. She pulled back. "There," she said. "I have sealed the past with a kiss. That means the past stays in the past. Do you agree Adam?"

Adam stared into the embers of the fire that now needed some attention. He stretched out and took some logs that were beside him. The fire took on new life as he threw the logs it began to sing a comforting, crackle song. Pouring himself some more champagne he then handed the bottle to Olivia who also filled her glass and she moved closer to him. He looked at Olivia as the light from the fire danced across her face. She was still as amazing as ever. She was still philosophical and positive, a quality not many people had. It was one of the things that he remembered her for. He had never met anyone who could be so happy and dance her way through life. He knew that no matter what he had to have her in his life once more.

CHAPTER SEVENTEEN

Adam was not going to let this chance slip away. He leaned in towards Olivia and began a long, slow, sensual kiss. A startled Olivia gave no resistance and began to melt under the warm softness of the lips she needed so badly. There is a moment in time when the earth stands still and this was it. A thousand thoughts run through a person's mind in seconds. This is followed by total emptiness and the place where thinking ends. The emptiness begins to fill with feelings unchained and life continues.

The moistness of their mouths met and their tongues danced in rapture. Euphoria settled over her and she abandoned herself to the tongue that was now probing and searching for hers. There were silent questions asked as their lips moved in unison and answers were ready to spill forth as their tongues conversed in a secret language of their own. Olivia melted into his arms and savoured the taste that was Adam. Her senses were enhanced by bergamot and lavender that permeated the air, the male smell, awakening that which had slept within her for years.

Without warning both pulled away from each other, startled by what had just happened and the reaction they both had to a closeness long forgotten. Adam and Olivia moved apart and stared out towards the ocean, one not daring to look at the other. Both gathering thoughts that were running crazed across their minds. Adam was wondering how far he should go, and Olivia was wondering where her resolve was. Confusion mixed with excitement slowly began to grow in Olivia as she waited for Adam's next move. Doubt and fear crowded Adam's mind, while he was considering what he should do next. He knew what he wanted to happen but something held him back. What was he afraid of? Why was he being indecisive? Was he afraid of rejection or that he might reignite his love for the woman he hurt so badly all those years ago?

Adam wanted this time, the night on the beach with the woman who came from the past. He wanted Olivia, now. He needed to grasp the moment. It would never come again.

Olivia lay back on the blanket. She looked at the stars and wondered what Adam was thinking. She began to wonder why he was not making a move on her. The alcohol was swimming in her veins, heat touching the parts that she wanted Adam to touch; she wanted him badly. She wanted more, much more. Olivia put her hand up and touched his sleeve. She whispered, "Adam." He heard his name despite the crashing of the surf. Adam turned and looked down at Olivia. She smiled. Those beautiful brown eyes speaking to him in a language that he understood. The smile and the eyes invited him to lay down beside her. Olivia was nervous and her mind began to wander. She smiled a wicked smile as Adam reminded her of Burt Lancaster in the film *Here to Eternity* when Burt dropped to his knees in one the most famous love scenes ever. The film's title came from a Rudyard Kipling poem called 'Gentleman Rankers' that was written in 1892.

Adam lay down beside Olivia and savoured the essence that surrounded her. He said, "You smell so lovely. You are so lovely." He thought, 'God, how can I be so cheesy?'

Olivia began to babble. "It is 'Believe' by Brittney Spears. I have used it for years. Lots of people tell me I smell nice. I can't buy it in the shops now. I have to get it from eBay or Amazon. It's not expensive." Olivia would have continued to babble had not Adam leaned over her and silenced her with another kiss. It was long and very slow. Each move of his tongue sent a spark of lust down to her yoni which awoke to the expectation of what might happen next.

After Olivia's earlier swim she had pulled on a loose top of blue and green. There was a large print of a butterfly on the back. It was one of her favourite tops and now it was being interfered with by Adam as he searched for the hem. Slowly his hand began to inch its way over Olivia's midriff. He found a breast that was warm and soft to the touch: beautiful.

Adam began to knead it gently coaxing the nipple to come alive. It wasn't long before Olivia lay naked before him. Adam jumped up and quickly undid his denim cut offs. His clothes were left redundant on the sand.

Olivia's eyes scanned his body. It was how she remembered it. His body was muscular and tanned. There were a few more hairs on his chest, black, speckled with grey. The years had been kind to Adam just as they had been kind to Olivia.

Olivia stretched and opened her legs wide. The invitation was sent and Adam accepted. He slowly began to internally massage Olivia with his magic wand. It wasn't long before Olivia's river overflowed, and spilled out onto the blanket leaving a wet stain that continued to grow. This night and the love making was perfection at its best. Making love in later years is like drinking a fine matured wine. There is softness and an awakening of senses not often used. There is less urgency as each sip is savoured. Sensations awaken giving rise to much appreciation. When younger, sex can be a bit like binge drinking, instant gratification and on to the next one.

What was happening on the beach was total sensuality, total erotica. As two became one, all the past was erased with one deep thrust as the orgasm went on and on. Adam spilled into Olivia with a deep moan and Olivia showered everywhere as she screamed with delight.

Later, holding each other on the beach, Adam and Olivia talked and talked. They began to make plans. They did not mention the past. There was no need. The picture of a bright future obliterated the last residue of that which had gone before. They were seen walking hand in hand along the beach by the water's edge as the sun was beginning to peep over the horizon. A perfect picture surrounded by an aura of happiness. They were oceans away from reality fixed in a dream of forever.

Olivia noticed the time on Adam's watch. "Oh my God, I need to go. Marcia will be here for me in an hour, and I have so much to do," she said.

Adam escorted her to her veranda and handed her the large lavender sweater that she forgot to pick up on the beach "Haven't I seen this before?" He asked. As she took the sweater from him, she replied, "Not this one, it was a pink one in 1987, same pattern." Adam's memory was stirred. Yes, a pink sweater that she never took off, he remembered. "We shall meet in New York. You have my card. Please call me when you have the time. I love you." Adam left Olivia with a kiss on her forehead, and she watched him as he walked away.

She entered the house and stood with her back against the door. Panic and anxiety soon got hold of her. What had she done? Why, oh why, had she let it get so far? This was not part of the plan for her future. This was madness. She began to cry tears of despair as she whispered, "No, no, no." Even the warm throbbing of her Venus mound reminding her of a wonderful experience, could not appease her.

Olivia showered quickly, threw all her belongs into her case and pulled on a black sweater and some black Capri pants. All she wanted to do was hide and black was a good colour to hide behind. Olivia locked the door behind her and walked up to the main highway. She did not look across at next door even though she could feel Adams eyes burning into her back. She just wanted to leave. She needed to sort herself out. She just needed to get back to work and not think about the night before at all. She carried her bags, and her gait was that of a little girl running away from home. She sat under a big tree by the roadside, out of sight of the houses on the beach and waited.

CHAPTER EIGHTEEN

An hour later, Olivia was sitting in the car next to Marcia. They were on Highway Nine and cruising at a good pace. When Marcia picked Olivia up, she was expecting the old vibrant Olivia to be there waiting for her. Instead, she found a morose and sad looking Olivia sitting on her suitcase with her head in her hands. Marcia sensed something was wrong and knew it was better not to ask. Olivia would speak in her own time. The radio played some good soul songs and they sped away from Cape May in silence listening to the harmonious tones of the Four Tops and The Supremes singing 'A taste of honey'. As the song ended an opening tear released a flood and Olivia cried. Heavy sobs were running from her soul. Her soul cried out to her, 'But he did come back for his honey and you.'

After a few hours they stopped at a cafe in a sheltered lay-by. They ordered croissants, hot chocolate with marshmallows and the waitress brought them a complimentary dish of late wild strawberries. Olivia began to tell Marcia about her week. She left out one part: the night before with Adam. Marcia said, "Well it sounds like you got what you needed." Olivia replied, "Well, did I?"

Marcia felt that Olivia was holding something back as her words did not match her body language at all and she was concerned about the way Olivia cried in the car. She told Marcia that the song always made her cry and there was nothing more to it. She sat a moment staring at the trees across the road before continuing. "You could say I got what I needed, and I also got more than I bargained for."

"Oh, you bought something then?" was Marcia's reply.

Olivia laughed a nervous laugh as she explained that it meant she got more than she had expected from her trip and it was nothing to do with shopping.

"Oh, I see, I think?" was the reply from Marcia that made Olivia laugh again and it seemed to break her mood.

She turned to Marcia and said, "Oh God Marcia, just when I think I have everything under control everything goes belly up."

"And belly-up means?" was Marcia's next question.

Olivia thought for a moment before saying, "Well it means upside down. Not wrong but more that something unexpected happens." She made a mental note to stop using idioms as it was sometimes hard to explain them.

Marcia looked quizzical and said, "And may I ask what went upside down err... belly-up?"

Olivia replied, "Well I did. I will tell you in the car. We best be off, or we won't be back before nightfall."

Olivia began to tell Marcia about Dino. How it surfaced to haunt her for some reason and that she had dealt with it. Now that was laid to rest. She went on to tell her about the flight over from England and her past with Adam and Felix. Marcia waited till the end and told Olivia she was proud of her and her new resolve to change her mindsets and move on.

Olivia went on. "That is not all. A person came to be next door yesterday. It was Adam."

"No way! Marcia said. "Do you think he followed you?"

"No not at all, he wouldn't have known where I was and if he did it doesn't matter now," Olivia replied. She went on to tell Marcia about the night on the beach. Marcia asked her what she was going to do. Olivia thought for a while and said, "Now I am going to get on a plane to Philadelphia. Go to the meeting you arranged and hopefully clinch a film deal. Yes, that's what I am going to do. I shall think about other things another time." That wasn't the answer Marcia expected and she saw the expression on Olivia's face that said the matter was closed.

CHAPTER NINETEEN

The next day found Olivia walking down a long corridor lost in the crowd of other travellers all making their way to the exit. Philadelphia airport was another huge space that needed careful navigation so as not to get lost. Olivia was in no rush and was soon on her own as the crowds left her behind. She looked at the black and white pictures on the wall that showed smiling faces of people unrecognised.

As she dragged her pink suitcase behind her, she noticed how sterile and shiny and colourless everything looked. Once out into the main hall Olivia looked around to find the exit. As she scanned the imposing room, she noticed a large bell. Olivia walked across to find it was made of grey and black Lego bricks. It was obviously meant to signify the liberty bell, which was all to do with American independence. It was quite something and Olivia wondered if she might find time to go and see the actual bell which she knew was located somewhere in a park. Olivia had read a lot about Philadelphia. She was a follower of Philadelphia soul from the sixties and seventies. She liked the cheese too, even though it came from New York. She really wanted to see as much as she could before the day ended.

Olivia's meeting with the film mogul was the next day and she had plenty of time on her hands. She had a lot of thinking to do about her week in Cape May. Whilst it seemed that her past was following her and she might never get rid of it completely, she felt a strange sense of freedom. Olivia was an independent woman and could do as she pleased. She had no ties except her little dog, Stanley. She hated leaving him when she went away. She never had a problem housing him as everybody wanted a piece of Stanley. Sometimes Olivia did not know what she wanted which made her a mass of inconsistencies. The feeling she carried just now made her think that perhaps she had cast off some baggage after all and she was finally leaving the chaos, she sometimes caused, behind her.

Olivia studied a large map standing by the exit to the airport. Soon she was making her way to Independence Hall. She went in search of the large bell with the crack in it and decided that today was a very good day. Walking into the reception hall Olivia could feel the historical residue left behind by days gone by.

Abraham Lincoln lay in state in this very building. The Declaration of Independence was signed here. The awesomeness of the rooms stirred a deep feeling within Olivia as she walked upon the boards that many famous people had walked on in past times. She made her way across to where the bell was housed. Here she was to see a piece of history symbolising slavery, oppression and freedom. The boards along the walls told the story of slaves, their plight and war; a compelling tale of pain and hope.

Olivia found herself in a group of tourists being hustled along. They stood and looked at the marvel before them. Next to Olivia there was a family that appeared to be from Japan. The father carried a large camera that was almost bigger than he was. Mum stood smiling in her silk, bright blue dress. Father began to push his children towards the bell. He obviously wanted to take a picture of them. He kept running backwards and forwards to reposition the children. He wanted a memorable photograph of their time in America. The two girls were smaller versions of their mother, also dressed in bright blue silk. The little boy was looking down at his feet; a look of defiance on his face. He did not want to have his picture taken. Dad shouted something and, as he clicked his Nikon, the little boy looked up and stuck a big fat tongue out. Olivia couldn't help herself and began to laugh. The little boy looked across at her, grinned and sent her a cheeky wink. Dad ran across to the children. He slapped the little boy and began to herd his brood away. He gave Olivia a very disgruntled look as they walked by. Olivia left the building with a smile on her face.

The afternoon sun was replaced by a grey hue as clouds moved quickly to blot out the bright blue of the afternoon. Olivia made her way to The Rittenhouse Hotel. A large black doorman greeted her. She thought, "I bet his grandparents were slaves" She made a mental note to speak to him about his history. There might be something for a book.

Soon Olivia was relaxing in a large bath full of bubbles. Candles lit and music playing she sipped her champagne. Just as she was drifting off into her dreams, Olivia's phone pinged. It was a text from Marcia.

You there yet? it said.

Olivia replied:

In the heart of luxury, thank you.

Unpacked and showered, Olivia switched on the television. She didn't pay much attention to it as her mind drifted back to the last night in Cape May. Her thoughts travelled to the beach and the man she left behind there. What was she to do? Olivia began to realise that she had never fully lost her love for Adam. He was the love of her life, he always was. She had never truly forgiven him for the way he behaved towards her at the end of their affair. It was obvious that he wanted to restart a relationship with her, he would not have asked her to ring him. It didn't much matter now. Mistrust of Adam and his words crept in. There was a saying, 'Once a cheat; always a cheat. Once a liar; always a liar. A leopard never changes its spots.' That night on the beach awakened something that she thought was long gone and now she had to deal with it as it was.

Olivia picked up the phone. A quaint voice answered, "Room service, what do you require?"

She thought for a moment. "I quite fancy some salmon and a glass of champagne," she said. "No perhaps I could do with a bottle please," she added. The lady at the end of the phone said she would have her order in five minutes. Olivia sometimes made rash decisions and was about to call back and change her order to one glass, not a bottle, when there was a knock at her door.

She opened the door to a bellboy holding a silver bucket containing a bottle of bubbly. 'Oh, what the heck!' she thought. After tipping the young man and determined to have just one drink Olivia placed the bucket on the table by the window. She poured herself a glass and watched the people below hurrying to who knows where. They were like ants on a mission making patterns on the pavement. Olivia needed to talk to someone, so she picked up the phone and rang Anne. England was about five hours in front so Olivia guessed that Anne would have just finished watching the soaps on TV. There was no reply. She didn't leave a message.

Pacing the floor, Olivia became restless as she couldn't shift the image from her mind of Adam on the beach in all his naked splendour. Her mind was full of questions without answers. She argued with herself until she found something to write on and began to write two lists. She wrote a positive list and a negative list as to why she should or should not rekindle a relationship with a man who almost destroyed her.

Olivia went through the night on the beach and the conversations they had. Adam never mentioned the word love. The night was purely in the moment although he had mentioned the future in a roundabout way. In hindsight Adam had used many words but hadn't really said anything at all except "Call me" when he left her by her front door. She had forgotten that he said "I love you."

Four drinks later, Olivia began to search for Adam's card. She went through everything to no avail. Sitting down on the sofa and in a moment of mind silence, Olivia heard a cynical voice. 'You stupid bitch, how did you forget? You threw his card into the ocean.' Well, that was that. The universe had once again taken her life into its hands. She was not meant to ring Adam, or the card would have been there. The decision was made for her.

Olivia didn't know whether to laugh or cry. She was slowly sliding down a pit of gloom when the phone rang and brought her back to the present. Anne said, "I missed your call. I was in the woods with the dogs. It is such a pleasant night here. Anyway, how are you? How was Cape May? Are you in New York yet?" Olivia explained that she was in

Philadelphia and that she had a meeting with a film director in the morning. Anne laughed, "I hope this is not another porn producer? Do they have beaches there?"

Olivia replied, "I don't know. I suppose so. I think there might be one about an hour away."

Anne said, "Steer clear then, you never know what might happen on a beach do you?"

Olivia couldn't decide if she should tell Anne about her encounter with Adam and what happened on the beach in Cape May. She went on, "Do you want another beach story?"

Anne replied, "Are you making one up?"

"No," said Olivia. "This one is true."

"Well of course I do. Just let me get a glass of wine and I am all yours." Olivia began to tell Anne about her last night in Cape May. She told all and left nothing out.

"When I couldn't get hold of you, I thought I might ring him, but I have thrown the number away."

There was complete silence. "Anne, are you still there?" Olivia asked.

Anne spoke, "yes I am here. Not often lost for words but just don't know what to say to you. What do you want to hear? You know what I think about that bastard. He tore my best friend apart, ruined her life and he will do it again. You had sex with him as well. I don't suppose condoms were involved either? I mean in all these years you wouldn't know where he's been! Well, what you do is your business. I love you and I am always here for you. Let's hope you don't catch anything from him."

Olivia began to panic as a teardrop rolled down her cheek. They talked for a bit longer and Olivia asked Anne what she thought she should do. "Well, there's nothing much you can do, is there, now you have thrown his number away? He could be anywhere. Listen to your heart or listen to your head. I think you need an early night. Pamper yourself and prepare for your meeting tomorrow. Forget him now. Leave him where he belongs, in your past and I'm sorry but I will always think of him as a bastard"

Olivia thought for a moment. "You are right, and I will. I love you," she said before putting the phone down.

The next morning Olivia was up with the larks. Dressed in her much-worn business suit she was ready to greet the day and clinch the deal. Adam was now firmly locked in the vault at the back of her mind. Back where he belonged, in history. On the stroke of nine, reception rang to say her car was waiting. As she stepped outside the hotel, Olivia saw a large black limousine. Surely it wasn't for her? She had never seen anything so black or so shiny. The driver who was waiting for her was shiny too. His bald head shone in the morning sunlight.

The black suit made him look rather like a funeral director not a chauffeur. He introduced himself as Moses. Olivia shook his hand and allowed him to escort her to the car. Once inside Olivia noticed the barrier glass that split the front from the back was closed. Olivia pulled it open and said, "Can't I sit up front with you, Moses?"

"More than my job's worth, madam," was the reply. Olivia sat back and smiled. Being called Madam, made her feel important. It reminded her of Vic in Myrtle Beach. She wasn't sure why as he called her 'Missy'.

Raising her eyes, she prayed, "Please let this be for real. Not a fiasco like the last time."

An hour later the car turned down a long avenue of cypress trees. In front of her Olivia could see a pink and white house, shining like a massive marshmallow in the bright daylight. It looked like a chateau with windows all around the bottom floor and brilliant white shutters at the upstairs windows. Pristine lawns of differing shades of green showered with the morning dew spread out forever. Olivia thought of the programme *Through the Keyhole* and heard the words, 'and who lives in a house like this?' She was looking forward to meeting the owner.

A large woman in a white apron came down the steps to greet her. She smiled and Olivia smiled back. The woman reminded her of a woman from southern American plantation days. She looked like she had just stepped off the film set for *Gone with the Wind*.

"Please come in, madam. My name is Hetty, and I am here to do your bidding," she said. Olivia followed Hetty through an ornate hallway that had the biggest crystal chandelier. It tinkled with the breeze coming through the house. They moved through a variety of rooms that were full of antiques and artefacts from other countries. Olivia followed Hetty into a conservatory that was filled with greenery and a rainbow of flowers. Hetty indicated that Olivia should sit at the table. She brought a platter full of meats, fruits and cheeses. Olivia did not realise how hungry she was and tucked in with a vengeance.

Hetty brought a variety of warm drinks and, before leaving, told Olivia that the master was making calls and would be joining her shortly. As Olivia finished her last croissant, she heard a shrill voice say, "And who are you?" She looked around and saw no one. Again, the voice said, "And who are you?" Still, she could see no one.

Feeling rather stupid she said, "I am Olivia and who are you?"

Out of the blue a large grey parrot landed on the table. It began to eye her suspiciously before saying, "And who are you?" Olivia laughed.

This seemed to put the bird at ease, and it began to eat the leftovers on her plate. "What's your name then? Olivia asked. "You certainly live in a beautiful place." The parrot ignored her. It was concentrating on breakfast and humans were stupid anyway.

The peace didn't last long as Olivia heard a shrill voice entering at the far end of the room. "Right, so have you got that? You can call him and tell him it's a deal." A very strange looking man entered between the tropical plants that framed the door. He was followed by a tall thin woman with thin black hair. She was obviously his PA. The man had an air of confidence about him, and he strode across the floor to greet Olivia. Olivia stood up.

"Olivia," he said. "I am so pleased to meet you. My name is Cornelius Jones. You may call me Corny, everybody else does." He laughed as he took hold of her hand and shook it with fervour.

It was the first time she had shaken hands with a wet fish. Corny's hand was sweaty and limp. Olivia tried not to laugh. This man, Corny Jones, was smaller than she was and looked like some type of internet geek. He turned to the thin woman and said, "Right Gertrude, you fetch the coffee and go make the rest of those calls. I do not want disturbing and tell Hetty that we shall lunch on the lawn today."

Olivia could not hide her grin. She thought, 'Gertrude! Gertrude and Corny? No way!' Cornelius Jones may have given a first impression of being an idiot but as the morning passed, he showed Olivia that he was no idiot but a very astute businessman.

After checking that Olivia had finished her breakfast Corny escorted her to his office. It was a stark contrast to the rest of the house and quite a surprise. Corny's office was bare, and the only real colour was the view out of one glass wall. There were rolling hills and horses in paddocks which looked more like a painting than reality. The other three walls were bare and white. In the middle of the room was a large trestle table and a bright red office chair. Olivia was wondering where she might sit when Corny pressed an invisible button on the wall and a large red velvet sofa slid out for them to sit on.

Corny noticed the look on Olivia's face and said, "Don't worry this is no casting couch. You are an attractive woman, but I am happy." He could see that Olivia had no idea what he meant, and he continued, "I do not like the word gay. It is a girl's name and also means happy. Thus, I am a happy man with no interest in women."

Olivia thought, 'I like him, already. He thinks like me.'

They settled down to have a long discussion about her book, *Chasing Rainbows*. Corny wanted to know everything about Olivia, her history and how she became a writer. Olivia was happy to give him all the information he asked for and answered his questions honestly. She went on to tell him that she was nearly at the end of the sequel. Corny was surprised as no one told him there was a second book in the pipeline. His intention was to do a one-off film ending with a cliff-hanger, but it looked like Olivia would not keep her readers guessing and had an ending in the second book, maybe?

He now began to wonder if a TV mini-series might be better suited to Olivia's story. Corny told her that he might change his mind about what they did with her story as it was all about money and what might bring in the biggest audience. "You have to send me the sequel as soon as it's done then," Corny said. "You will stay for lunch, won't you? Please? I have some people who would like to meet you." Olivia asked who they were and was told they were the financial backers and were putting up the money for the project if they came to an agreement and signed a contract.

Lunch was very successful, and the rest of the day passed very quickly. Before Olivia left, she shook hands with a few people knowing that the deal was done. Corny was very pleased and said that he would liaise with Marcia and the lawyers and that she would receive contracts for signing in a couple of weeks. This meant that Olivia would have to stay in America longer than anticipated but she did not mind. She was still in shock about the whole day and the wonderful outcome. This was really happening to her now. Her first book was to become a film or even a mini-series. Her dream was coming true and, when she left, she looked back at the pink and white marshmallow house. She spoke to two people who could not hear her. She said, "Well, Adam and Felix, if only you knew. You both dumped me in a pile of shit and I have come up smelling of roses."

CHAPTER TWENTY

On her return from Philadelphia Olivia found herself thinking of home. She had a few more weeks left and then she would be on her way back to Manchester airport. Five weeks in America and a few more to go before she could return to the comfort of her cottage close to the Yorkshire Moors. She wasn't sure what to think about the emotional roller coaster ride that began on the flight over. She knew she still had lots of thinking to do. Olivia needed to process all that had happened so far and get back on the right track. She'd been comfortable and content with her life and now Adam and Felix had rattled her cage. She prayed that they would not be on the flight back. It was easy to become paranoid about such things.

Olivia's trip to Philadelphia was a great success and she had so much to look forward to. Marcia was waiting for her at the airport with details of the 'award' night. Olivia would gain acknowledgement for her work and all the charity work that she had done in the past. Olivia never thought about awards and recognition when she began to write. Writing was something she had always wanted to do but had no time when she worked. Now, in her retirement, it was a full-time job. For years Olivia's friends and students urged her to write but she never had the confidence.

Now she had fame and a film deal. Olivia was an advocate of writing. She felt it was good for the soul. It was a cleansing experience to read one's thoughts and words on paper. A therapist will tell a person to keep a journal for good reason. Feelings on paper helped unload unwanted baggage, the type of baggage that stops a person moving on with their life. Baggage that ties them to their past or even their present, which might be loaded with guilt, regrets and a mountain of 'if onlys'. It can be hard to push memories aside. They are there for a reason and resurface without invitation. They may hang around until dealt with and then may be filed in the back of the mind in a file labelled 'Dealt With'.

As Olivia looked at herself in the mirror she smiled, feeling that she dealt with her baggage many moons ago and was now ready to move on. She touched her cheek and felt cleansed and free. A knock on the door startled her and brought her back from her mind wanderings. She skipped across the room. She was truly in the moment. Marcia was standing behind a bellboy who was holding a large bunch of lilacs and sunflowers.

They were just like the ones she received when she first arrived in America. "Good grief," she said. "Surely these can't all be for me?"

The bellboy replied, "They sure are and this bottle of champagne." Olivia had failed to notice the trolley with the ice bucket holding a large green bottle. The bellboy tipped his cap. Olivia tipped the boy.

Marcia asked, "Shall we open it now?"

"Why not!" was the reply.

Marcia continued, "Someone is certainly sending you a message. There wasn't a card the first time. Maybe there is one now," she said as she began to carefully look through the flowers. She found a small pink envelope and handed it to Olivia. Olivia placed it on the table and continued to put on her lipstick. "Aren't you going to open it?" Marcia asked.

Olivia turned and replied, "Oh, it can wait but if you are interested why don't you open it?"

Marcia was a genuinely inquisitive person. She would have made a good private detective. As a child she would always find her Christmas presents before the day and then had to feign surprise. She couldn't help herself. Inside the pink envelope was a folded piece of pink paper. The message was neatly typed, so whoever sent them must have ordered by phone. The message was the words of a song, 'Oceans Away' by Phillip Goodhand Tait.

"Well," Marcia remarked. "This is a mystery, unless you know who it is?" Olivia shook her head and went to open the champagne. Meanwhile Marcia pulled her phone out and soon 'Oceans Away' was playing. Olivia and Marcia sat on opposite sofas. Neither spoke till the song finished. Olivia had a strange look on her face. Marcia said, "I never heard that song before, it sure is beautiful. You know who sent the flowers don't you."

Before Olivia could answer, the phone began to ring. As Marcia stretched over to pick up the receiver Olivia gave a sharp, "Don't!"

The answer machine kicked in and a deep sexy voice spoke. "Hope you like the flowers. I'm not oceans away. Call me please. I want to see you. Please Olivia, call." The click of the receiver at the other end echoed round the room.

Olivia spoke, "That was Adam."

"Wow, what a voice! Are you going to call him?" she asked.

A curt reply of "No" told Marcia to drop the subject and not ask anything else.

Olivia switched the television on as she said, "Time to catch up with the world, me thinks. We have half an hour to spare." Out of the blue and without warning Olivia then said, "I threw his number away. I am moving forward and not going backwards."

An air of melancholy descended on them as they watched how bad things were and how the weather was causing havoc. Olivia and Marcia began to solve all the problems of the world and laughed when Marcia asked, "Should I stand for president?"

Ruby Andrews began to sing 'Just Loving You' in the bedroom and Olivia went in search of her mobile, which was ringing relentlessly. She didn't recognise the number and prayed it wasn't Adam. A chirpy cockney voice surprised her.

"Olivia, is that you?" a young man asked.

Olivia laughed. "Depends on who's calling."

"Wayne Stringer," was the reply. The silence was broken as he continued, "We met in Central Park a few weeks ago."

Olivia laughed again, "Oh yes, of course. How are you, Wayne?"

"I'm good." He continued, "I know it is short notice, but I wondered if you would like to come out with me and the gang tonight?"

Olivia looked across at Marcia and mouthed, "Do you fancy going out tonight?" Marcia nodded. "Yes Wayne," was the reply. "Marcia and I would love to come out with the gang. Where are we going?"

"It's speakeasy night at Raines Law Room," Wayne carried on.

Olivia mouthed "Raines Law Room?" to Marcia. Marcia jumped up and down nodding. Olivia asked Wayne what time and how they would get there. Wayne said he would meet them in the foyer of the hotel at nine p.m.

As Olivia ended the call Marcia grinned. "You will love it there. We will have to dress the part though."

"What do you mean?" asked Olivia. Marcia told Olivia that Raines Law Room was rather famous and like a 1920's speakeasy. Olivia became caught up in Marcia's excitement and forgot all about Adam as they left the room to go to the awards ceremony.

After a late lunch amongst literary people and writers, Marcia and Olivia made their way to Vintage Textiles. Marcia complimented Olivia on her award acceptance speech. "I can't believe you did not have anything written down. Most people I have seen make notes." Olivia told her that the notes were in her head. She did lots and lots of thinking instead. It was best to see what the audience was like and to speak from the heart. Notes could be helpful, but it could go very wrong trying to follow notes that did not match an audience.

Public speaking was Olivia's forte and if she had not become a writer, perhaps she would have been an after-dinner speaker. Marcia asked, "May I ask you a personal question please Olivia?"

Olivia said, "Fire away."

Marcia went on, "Why do you sometimes act like a complete airhead when you are obviously so intelligent and clever?" She was surprised by Olivia's reply.

"Because I can."

The rest of the afternoon was spent in the dress agency trying on dresses amidst lots of giggles and laughter. Champagne was drunk and they were both having a good 'girly time'. Olivia picked a cream, beaded chiffon, flapper dress that was embellished with sparkly beads in a cobweb design. It fitted perfectly and was extremely flattering. She also chose some silk embroidered shoes with a small heel. Marcia also chose a cream flapper dress. It was not as 'bling' as Olivia's and made of Irish lace. Both outfits complemented the other. Olivia persuaded Marcia not to go home. The friends returned to the hotel to get ready.

She linked arms with Marcia and dragged her up the steps of the Trump International saying, "I shall be going home in a couple of days so let's spend as much time as we can together."

Marcia said, "Yes, OK but I won't be sharing a bed with you." They both giggled. They showered and dressed. Each did the other's hair. Olivia ordered a meal of salmon and fries and they settled down with a jug of gin and tonic to wait for Wayne.

The conversation returned to Adam, and Marcia saw that Olivia still had lots of thinking to do. Olivia began the conversation, which confused Marcia as she was told that they would not bring 'that man' up again. Olivia took a call from Cornelius Jones who was ringing to see if the contracts had arrived. Olivia's mobile began to sing and Marcia answered. It was Anne. "Is that Marcia?" a chirpy voice said.

"Yes," was the reply.

Anne continued, "Hi, it's Anne. I am sure you know all about me because I know a lot about you."

Marcia said, "Yes and it's nice to be speaking to you. Olivia is just on the other line do you want to leave her a message."

"No," Anne said. "I was wondering how she is, that's all? Did she tell you about Cape May?"

"Yes, she did," was Marcia's reply.

Anne continued, "I worry about her. I don't think she is over him. What do you think?"

Marcia thought for a moment. "Well, she says she is. I think she needs to come home now and put everything behind her."

"So do I," said Anne. "Been nice talking to you. Please tell her I shall call tomorrow."

Marcia said, "Likewise." As Marcia put the phone down Olivia returned to the room.

"Was that Anne?" she asked.

The reply was "Yes."

Olivia went on, "Was she fussing?"

Marcia nodded.

CHAPTER TWENTY-ONE

It was a warm evening and at nine precisely, there were two gorgeous ladies sitting in reception waiting for their escort. Their hair hidden under beaded cloche hats and their cream dresses flapping round their knees made them look as though they had just stepped out of the 1920s. At one minute past nine Wayne walked through the door. He was wearing a black dinner suit. A white wing collar over a red spotted bow tie and black and white spats. With his hair slicked back, he looked gorgeous and every bit the gangster. He kissed both ladies on the cheek before handing both of them a pink camellia corsage.

Olivia introduced Marcia to Wayne. It was instant karma as Wayne took Marcia's hand and held it to his lips. Olivia saw the sparks fly as their eyes met. After more than a minute which seemed like an hour, Olivia said, "So are we going out or are you two going to stand staring at each other all night?" Wayne pulled himself away from Marcia's eyes, apologised and gave his arm to each of the ladies. They were a sight to behold as they swanked out of reception. Olivia danced with glee when she saw the Ford model A Sedan waiting for them by the kerb.

"Wow," Olivia said. "You do know how to wow, don't you?"

On the way to Raines Law Room, Wayne gave the ladies a history lesson about the 1920s and prohibition. Olivia said, "I remember them."

Wayne said, "You can't possibly you aren't that old."

Olivia laughed. "Yes, I do, it was *The Roaring Twenties* on TV when I was a little girl." They all laughed. Marcia didn't ask any questions or say anything. She just kept taking sneaky looks at Wayne, the whole time.

When they arrived at the bar, a bouncer took the keys off Wayne and drove the car away. They walked down some narrow steps in single file to a shiny door with a brass bell at the side. "Are you sure we are in the right place?" Olivia asked. Wayne nodded as he rang the bell. A small hatch opened, and two eyes peered out at them.

'OMG!' thought Olivia. 'This is just like *The Untouchables*.' As they entered the room the jazz of the past met their ears. The place was half empty. Wayne assured them that the bar would fill up later. He explained that his gang always came early so as to get a decent seat as later there would be nowhere to sit. Wayne led them down the room, past a long bar to a row of green leather chesterfields. Similarly dressed people waved at Wayne as they passed.

They reached the end of the bar and a group of people made space for Wayne and the two women. After introductions to those already there, Olivia sank into the corner of one of the sofas with her back to the wall so she could see the whole room. She thought she might get some material for a book if she could see everybody. The music played on, and Olivia drifted back into an era that she had always admired.

Olivia whispered to Marcia, "Do you think Elliott Ness or Dorothy Provine might appear?"

Marcia looked at her. "Who?" she asked.

"Oh, never mind," Olivia dismissed the question with a wave of her hand as she began to observe her surroundings. Wayne asked them what they would like to drink. Olivia was feeling reckless and told him that she would drink whatever he brought. "Surprise me," she said. She turned to Marcia saying, "Let's make this a night to remember, a real party night."

While they waited for their drinks Olivia studied the decor before holding up her hand and whispering behind it, "Marcia have you seen the wallpaper?"

Marcia looked. "Nice pattern," she observed.

"No," Olivia said. "Look closer."

Marcia looked closer and her hand came up to her mouth. "Oh, they are silhouettes of people in sexual positions, making love." Their eyes met and they burst out laughing.

It wasn't long before Wayne returned with a tray of posh looking cocktail glasses. Olivia took one as she said, "Well I know I will drink anything, but it would be nice to know what anything is." Wayne obliged by telling them it was called a Marie Antoinette. It consisted of white rum, raspberries, lemon and crème de cacao drizzled over crushed ice.

Olivia took a sip as Wayne asked her, "You certainly going to party tonight then?"

He received a wicked grin followed by a wink as Olivia replied, "I certainly am. Watch this space."

The bar began to fill up and Olivia saw why they had come early. It became more than full, as people pushed their way to the bar which was absolutely crowded. Olivia chatted to those around her as Marcia and Wayne got to know each other better. They were practically oblivious to their surroundings as they got deeper and deeper into conversation. After bringing more drinks and a bucket containing three bottles of wine Wayne told them that later they would go to The Groove. He said it was the only place in New York where a person could hear live R & B, funk and soul. Olivia asked, "So will there be dancing?" Wayne nodded.

The place was getting noisier, and a person had to shout to be heard. Olivia was happy and getting rather merry after three Marie Antoinette's. It didn't stop her drinking the wine though. It looked like she might be drunk before she went home. This really was like a speakeasy from the 1920s. It reminded Olivia of when her boys appeared in *Bugsy Malone* at their local theatre. It was many moons ago and so much water had passed under the bridge now.

A quiet space opened inside of her as she thought of the love, she had for them. She shook her head. She was not going to do any more thinking. It was party night and she was going to enjoy her last few days in New York. The storyteller in Olivia began to wonder when the gangsters would appear.

She didn't have to wait long. The outer door opened as a group of people left and another group entered. Olivia could not believe her eyes. The gangsters appeared. Across the room she saw Adam and Felix together with two women walking in behind them that could only be described as aging bimbos with false breasts. Olivia felt her heart pounding as though it would soon leap out of her chest.

The women reminded her of the Dolly sisters from the TV programme *Mr Selfridge*. Olivia downed her drink and asked for another one. Wayne refilled it and was startled when Olivia finished it off in one gulp. He decided that this lady definitely knew how to party. She leaned over to Marcia and said, "Have you seen who just walked in at your eleven o' clock?"

Marcia looked across the floor and replied, "Two men, one is bald, and the other is dark and gorgeous. They are with two women." Olivia forgot that Marcia didn't know what Felix and Adam looked like. Marcia saw only faces that she did not recognise.

"It is Adam and Felix, and they are together!"

"Oh no," said Marcia. She took a longer look and took more notice. "Who are the women?"

"I have no idea," Olivia said.

"What are you going to do?" Marcia asked.

"Easy," said Olivia. "I am not going to do anything. I told you I am over him and moving on."

Marcia nodded and said, "Oh right." She thought to herself, 'Are you? Are you really? You don't look it to me.'

The evening continued and a girl singer came on stage. She was covered head to foot in indigo sequins and looked every bit the star. She sang a medley of songs including 'You do Something to me', 'Don't bring Lulu' and many more songs from a bygone era. Olivia's passion was music. She always had her headphones on and was rather knowledgeable on most genres. The set ended and Olivia went to speak to the singer who had entertained so well. As she walked across the room, she noticed Adam, Felix and the false breasted women huddled together in a corner. They looked to be having the time of their lives.

As Olivia looked on, she felt something ignite in the pit of her stomach. What was it? Surely, she wasn't jealous? Just, as she was about to look away, Adam looked up and their eyes met. Olivia read the look that ran across Adam's face. It said, 'I've been sussed'. She was rarely wrong. Olivia found the feeling in her stomach turning into a full-blown panic attack. She looked round the room. She had to get out. She was feeling like a cornered wild animal. She returned to Marcia and Wayne and picked up her bag.

"Marcia, I am just going for some fresh air."

She saw a door leading to a small courtyard and disappeared through it very quickly. There was no escape from the courtyard. No door to the outside world. Olivia sat down at a table and put her head in her hands. A waiter came and asked her if she wanted a drink, and she ordered a whisky. She stopped him, "Make that a double, please." As she waited for her drink, Olivia began to gather her thoughts. The panic began to subside and was replaced by an emotion that she said she never experienced as it was a waste of time.

Olivia spoke to the whitewashed brick wall in front of her. She said, "Am I jealous? Am I really jealous?" The realisation startled her and the voices in her head began to argue. They laughed at her, causing her anxiety to grow. "No, no," she said. "I can't be jealous. He means nothing to me." The white wall stood silent.

The voice in her head spoke, 'He's always meant something to you. He did in Cape May! You gave him your body, your love, your everything!'

CHAPTER TWENTY-TWO

Olivia's drink arrived. As the waiter turned to leave the courtyard, Olivia downed it in one and called him back. She ordered another. She was just on the sober side of drunk now and began to get angry. "How dare they?" she asked the whitewashed wall beside her. "Of all the bars in New York they had to come into this one."

Olivia had not expected to see Adam ever again. She certainly had not expected to see him with Felix and the Dolly sisters' daughters. She began to giggle, "What if they were related to the Dolly sisters after all? Or maybe they were the actresses that played them in *Mr Selfridge*?"

Olivia's mind began to run riot with chaotic thoughts of 'what ifs'. Her new-found jealousy and anger were fusing to make one almighty bomb ready to explode. What if Adam had now told Felix about his affair with her? What if they had compared notes and laughed? What if she had not slept with Adam in Cape May? What if she hadn't fallen into his arms? What if she had said to him all the things that were stored and rehearsed over the years just in case, she saw him again? She had seen him again and she said nothing.

She was not regretting the night with Adam. She had not been made love to like that for many a year or maybe longer. She knew that it would not go anywhere and that it was a rare occurrence; oceans away from Yorkshire. She made the decision that the encounter on the beach was a one off. There was no future for her and Adam. Olivia had taken control of her life and walked away from Adam. Yet here he was again. What was the universe doing to her?

She began to think about the men she met after her divorce. How vulnerable she was and what an idiot she became. It was so easy to be led up the garden path when looking for love. It was hard when one had to wake up and smell the roses to find they were only weeds. Sometimes Olivia was her own worst enemy.

A person had to take some responsibility for what happens in their life. The problem was that Olivia always blamed herself and it was easier to walk away than confront the issue and speak her mind. She was good at making excuses for bastards. A lot of women do it.

Olivia called for another drink and realised that she must make this her last as she slurred her order and tried to stop a hiccup. She stared at the painted wall. It was not moving so that was a good sign. She really had to get a grip, or she might not be able to walk back inside and keep her dignity intact. Olivia began to fool herself into thinking that perhaps Adam had not seen her. Their eyes had met, he looked right into her soul and made the butterflies in her stomach flip over.

She slowly began to manage her breathing. A calmness began to wash over her as she regained control of her mind and the whisky began to do its job. The thoughts in her head began to fade and peace slowly crept in. She jumped when a hand tapped her on the shoulder. The dark deep tones of a voice she knew so well tiptoed into her ears. "May I join you?" Adam sat down next to Olivia without invitation and began to speak. "Hello, I thought you might have rung me? I hope you got the flowers? Olivia, I meant every word I said on the beach."

Olivia wanted Adam to go away but she knew he wouldn't. She took a drink and coughed. The alcohol hit her in the head as it hit her stomach. Now she had gone over the limit and she knew it. With the realisation that she was drunk also came the courage she needed.

"Why are you here Adam? Why can't you leave well alone? Won't those women and Felix wonder where you are? You all having a foursome later?" Olivia felt her anger and jealousy returning with a vengeance fuelled by the whisky. "You just can't help it can you? What a womaniser! You want me to ring you and then I see you with those... those women!" She raised her hand and made a full sweep before her. Adam couldn't help laughing, "You're not jealous are you, Olivia?"

Olivia was on a roll, and she stopped herself just before the tears began. One escaped and didn't go unnoticed by Adam. He did not know whether to laugh. He thought better of it as he had never seen Olivia like she was now.

He held up his hand. "Woah! Just a minute, just a minute," he said. "I am doing Felix a favour. They are his cousins and he hasn't seen them in years. There is nothing funny going on."

Olivia scowled and replied, "Yep and Father Christmas comes at Easter." Olivia caught the waiter's eye and asked for another drink.

Adam asked, "Don't you think you have had enough?"

Olivia retorted, "What's it got to do with you?" She stopped the waiter before he left and said, "Please bring me a mug of black coffee and a glass of water with that." It was time for Olivia to take control before she said something she might regret later.

Adam ordered a double brandy as he felt he might need it. Olivia turned to him. "Am I supposed to believe you? I believed you all those years ago, so you, tell me why I should? You took my heart and you crushed it. You destroyed me and you think I don't know what you did?"

Adam continued to listen to Olivia in her rant and, when he could, he managed to say, "I think you have lots to say to me. I will listen but wonder why you didn't say it in Cape May?"

Olivia continued, "So do I, but Cape May was a dream, a diversion. I have come to my senses, and you have again shown your true colours. Yes, I have lots to say to you Adam but what's the point. It's all too late. Too much time has passed. I have nothing to say to you but, goodbye." Adam did not move. The people at the next table left the courtyard and they were completely alone. The sad words of the singer inside drifted out to them. Olivia could not bear the silence and she did not want to hear the singer, who continued to roll about in her heart with such sad words.

The pressure was leading up to the tears that were now gathering. She must keep control. She would not let this man see her cry. The sadness of the song which was 'If I ain't got you', sung by Alicia Keys, who was one of Olivia's favourite singers, was soon replaced by an anger that would not disappear. The waiter returned with a tray of drinks and nibbles. Olivia gave a smile that she did not mean and asked him to close the door behind him as she could no longer bear the singing.

Olivia downed the water before her and turned to Adam as she picked up the coffee cup, she knew this would be her last chance ever to say all the things stored up inside. It was now or never. She turned on Adam like a woman possessed. She did not shout and scream like some women might. Olivia spoke very slowly and clearly. This was not her, but a woman scorned, and she was about to unleash all her unhappiness and resentment for the last time.

"I put my marriage on the line for you. I jeopardised everything and then left the marriage anyway as I was so scared my husband would eventually find out. He did in the end and it must have hurt him terribly. I can't put that right. We hurt so many people by what we were doing even though they did not know. I trusted you. You told me you loved me. She sipped her coffee before continuing.

"You probably loved the idea of me. You picked me up at a bad time in my life. I lost my job. My son was ill, and I needed an escape from all the pressure. You were my saviour. Without you, who knows what I might have done. I was foolish to believe you. We were both diversions from our crap lives. We thought we had it all and we had nothing. When you dumped me the first time, I was practically suicidal. I so wanted to hate you, but I couldn't. I got so stuck in my life until my friend told me to go see her friend as she thought I might need some regression therapy. Seemingly we sometimes get stuck in the lives before now."

Olivia laughed. "God, that sounds so stupid now, but desperate people do desperate things. You won't want to listen to this."

Adam replied, "Yes I do, please go on."

Olivia continued, "It isn't nice and truly unbelievable. You won't believe it." Olivia sighed and took a drink of the coffee that was cooling. "The lady was called Betty and lived in Cleckheaton. She explained what she would be doing and took me upstairs to a small room with a bed and a box of tissues in it. She took me to three past lives, and it was fascinating. It all seemed to make sense. She took me back to the life before this. I was a farm girl in France called Francine. I was about fifteen. I was raped by some soldiers and one of them had me when I had gone into the light. Dead, you know. He didn't want to, but his friends jeered him on." She looked closely at Adam before continuing.

"Betty told me that I held no malice and felt only compassion for that person. Later the young soldier hung himself. Betty then said, 'And this person is known to you now.' I knew instantly that it was you. There was no doubt in my mind and that was why I could not hate you. You should have been hated and all I could do was love you." Adam looked down at his hands as Olivia went on. "Can you remember when it was your fortieth birthday and I sent you that card written in French? Why do you think I did that Adam? Because I don't know. At the time I thought I might embarrass you as you don't know French and would have to ask someone who did. Ask what the words meant."

Adam nodded. "I remember and it said, '*Jet'aime toujours*'. I love you always." Adam shook his head and said, "I am sorry."

He should have kept his sorry to himself as it served to unleash the beast in Olivia. The lion within roared and she continued in a much louder voice this time. "Sorry! Sorry! What have you got to be sorry about? You got what you wanted. You got your thrills and kicks out of me. You left me for my friend." The venom was aimed. "You left me for that woman who said she was my friend. That made me a bigger bitch as I was friends with your wife."

Olivia felt the tears stinging and she made a conscious effort to keep them in check. She was never going to cry because of this man again. She went on. "And then when your wife was going to leave you! What about then? You betrayed me. You told her about us. Why? What purpose did it serve? Just you getting revenge on her. I never did you any wrong did I? Did you compare bed notes with Felix?" Olivia wiped the tears that were now in full flow as she continued, "after that terrible phone conversation with you, my life turned a corner. It turned into absolute chaos and remained that way for years. I loved you so much." She wiped a hand across her face and waited for an answer.

Adam felt so bad and continued to look away from Olivia. He shook his head. By this time, she was not thinking straight as all her hurt came pouring out and she got more abusive as she continued to let Adam know just how he destroyed her and the mayhem he caused. Olivia did not look at him as she finished her coffee. She had now said what needed to be said and that was the end of it. She rose to go to the toilet and turned to say, "I couldn't have rung you anyway. I threw your card away."

Adam saw that she left her bag behind and slipped another of his cards into it. When she returned Adam sighed before saying, "I deserved that. I am so sorry."

Like a red rag to a bull the words infuriated Olivia. She looked down at her hands as she said, "Oh, why don't you just fuck off Adam. I don't know what you want, and I don't think I care. Just fuck off!" Olivia turned to look at Adam hoping he would get up and walk away. He sat before her silently with tears rolling down his cheeks. He was a broken man.

Olivia felt terrible now. Why had she done this when all she needed to do was walk away from him? But she had wanted to hurt him as he hurt her. Olivia had succeeded in her wish. Adam did not stop crying. Olivia sat staring at him. She had not expected him to cry. She wasn't sure how she was feeling apart from, more than drunk. A few minutes passed, they seemed like a lifetime, before Adam began to speak. "Did Cape May mean nothing to you? It meant everything to me. I won't go over old ground. We both know what was said up there and as far as I am concerned it still stands. I deserved every word you just threw at me and more. I cannot turn the clock back Olivia, but I can do right by you now, if you will let me." Olivia waited for Adam to continue. "I will not forget what I did to you. I can make amends. It is obvious that you have drunk far too much and will probably forget what you said in the morning. I won't. Please take some time to remember the things we said on the beach. We were happy to have found each other again. I was so disappointed that you ran off the next morning, but I understood. I need to go now. Please call me when you are in a rational mood and sober. Enjoy the rest of your evening." Olivia did not look at Adam. She stared in front of her at the white wall. Adam rose and kissed her on the top of her head before returning inside. She turned quickly to see the door closing behind him.

Olivia finished her drink before throwing the glass at the wall. Adam's words and the shattering glass helped to sober her up, a little. She began to hear words in her head that were loud and clear. 'Why do I feel like a naughty girl who has been told off? Why should I care and feel so jealous and angry?' The answer was a simple one. She still loved him. She had never stopped loving him. All these years she had lied to herself in order to keep her sanity. Now this was all becoming insane.

Olivia re-entered the bar. She pushed her way through the crowd and found Marcia and Wayne. They were still gazing at each other and holding hands now. They looked so loved up. Olivia sat down heavily beside them. Marcia looked up, "Are you all right Olivia?" she asked. Olivia nodded, not trusting herself to speak. Wayne ordered more drinks and soon Olivia began to emerge from the pit that she had been kicked into by emotions best left alone.

Marcia leaned over to Olivia and said, "I really like Wayne. You look awful."

This was the prompt Olivia needed to go to the washroom and tidy herself up. As she crossed the room, she found that she was looking for Adam and his party. They were nowhere to be seen. Olivia splashed her face with cold water and as she patted herself dry, she looked in the mirror and spoke. She said, "Now, come on girl move on up and keep on keeping on."

She smiled as she remembered the Northern Soul of days gone by. As she left the room she turned and winked at herself in the mirror. This was party night, and she was going to party. Tomorrow was another day and as far as she was concerned Adam was definitely history now.

CHAPTER TWENTY-THREE

A few hours later Wayne, Marcia and Olivia were dancing to Block Party at The Groove. All thoughts of Adam vanished as Olivia lost herself in the music and Marcia and Wayne lost themselves in each other. The drink and dancing took its toll on Olivia. The emotions that had played havoc with her earlier left her exhausted. She was feeling like a gooseberry as she sat beside Marcia and Wayne, who would not have noticed a bomb drop or the roof fly off, they were so engrossed. Instant love is a wonderful thing and these two were more than instant.

Olivia noticed the door open across the room and got the biggest surprise of her life. In walked one of Olivia's best friends. Their eyes met and they both laughed. She got up and ran through the dancers. They wrapped their arms around each other and hugged as best friends do. Olivia said, "I can't believe this! What on earth are you doing here, Harry?"

Harry Greenman was her alter ego. They were so alike and spent such good times together in the past on the Northern Soul scene. Harry told Olivia that he was taking a few days out with his newest girlfriend. Her name was Betsy. Olivia laughed. "What sort of a name is that? I have a friend with a dog called Betsy."

Harry raised a finger to his lips. "Shh… here she comes." A tall slim woman with blonde hair hanging to her waist tottered across the room, in heels that were ridiculous and made her look nine feet tall. Harry introduced them and they shook hands politely. Betsy looked down her nose at Olivia who began to feel uncomfortable under the hostile stare.

A common squeaky voice said, "So you are the famous Olivia. Hey?" she nodded towards Harry, "never stops talking about you; his famous friend!" Olivia looked up at Betsy who was at least a foot taller than her and wondered if Betsy could see where Olivia's hair was thinning on top. Olivia self-consciously stroked the top of her head. Sometimes she did not like this ageing thing. Hair moved about your body and began to grow in strange places. The hair on Olivia's legs were now sprouting on her top lip. Thank goodness for waxing. At least she wasn't getting those straggly 'pubic hairs' that some women begin to sprout on their chin.

The two friends sat down together, and Harry ordered some drinks. Not that he needed any more as he was way past merry and well on his way to being on another planet. Olivia laughed and thought, 'Please don't ever change my friend.' Before long, a short tubby redhead joined them. Harry introduced her as Betsy's friend, Angel. She looked more like a ginger cherub than an angel.

Just as Olivia was beginning to wonder why Harry always went for blondes who were taller than he was, Harry and Betsy got up to dance. Even when drunk Harry was master of the dance floor, and it wasn't long before he was strutting his stuff to an audience that were appreciating his mastery. He moved as if on hovercraft shoes to the beat of Bobby Womack singing 'Home is where the Heart is'.

Olivia turned to Angel and began a conversation which did not last long, as it appeared that Angel was low on vocabulary. It consisted of 'yes, no and dunno.' Without warning Angel jumped up as Ace Spectrum began to sing 'Don't send nobody else'.' She ran onto the dance floor. It was obvious that she was a hand bagger. A hand bagger is someone who would like to be a Northern Soul person but just can't help dancing round their handbag and wears clothes that do not reflect the culture of soul. Betsy began stepping and was totally out of synch with the music. It was a sight to behold. As Angel and Betsy got into the groove, Harry took the opportunity to return and chat to Olivia. "She is very like the Amazon, isn't she?" Olivia commented and smiled.

The Amazon was a woman that Harry could not get rid of years ago, when he and Olivia first met. He finished with the Amazon and went through a few months of hell with her.

"Oh my God, Oli," Harry always called Olivia, Oli, it served to make her one of the boys. "How come you remember so far back? I could not get rid of her. She wanted to get engaged, do you remember? She wanted a thirty-five grand diamond ring and I'd only been going with her for four months."

Olivia said, "Your own fault, Harry, you always had to tell them about your money and how you were king of the laundrettes. Didn't you?"

Harry went on, "Can you remember I had to send her an email telling her to fuck off. She didn't and I had to send her another one saying, 'what part of fuck off don't you understand?' She got fed up with stalking me when she found another victim."

They both began to laugh as they went through their memories of times gone by. They discussed the bunny boiler and how hard that was for them both as she blamed Olivia for their split and began to bad mouth both Harry and Olivia on the soul scene.

"We had some laughs and some tears, didn't we Harry? So, what's with this one? When are you going to get one you can look straight in the eye?" Olivia asked. Harry wasn't big in stature, but he was big in personality and kindness and that is what matters, not the inches.

Harry replied, "I felt sorry for her. Someone dumped her at The Blackpool weekender, and I picked up the pieces."

"Two of them I think," Olivia added as she nodded across at Angel.

"Well, you never know Oli, she might be up for a threesome, and I am here for a good time and not a long time," Harry laughed and winked.

Olivia laughed as she replied, "Yes right, they would eat you alive my friend. You might disappear up a dark hole never to be seen again." The time passed quickly and as day began to dawn, they all said their goodbyes and returned to their respective hotels.

Betsy did not say goodbye to Olivia as she marched off down the street shouting impatiently, "Come on Harry." Harry shrugged his shoulders at Olivia and after giving her a swift peck on the cheek ran off after the two women who were about to turn a corner. Olivia smiled to herself as she shook her head, thinking 'God love him. He thinks he is here for a good time and not a long time and I am here for a good time and a long time.'

At some point in the evening Olivia sent Anne a text telling her about Adam and Felix. Her phone now pinged, and she read the reply from her dear friend. Then she quickly tapped back.

I will be home soon, and things will go back to normal. What an adventure this has been. Don't want another one for quite some time. Need some peace and to rest. Love you xxx

It was four in the morning when Olivia, Marcia and Wayne were sipping coffee in Olivia's hotel suite. Olivia told them about her encounter with Adam and that she had well and truly finished it now. She would not be seeing Adam again. That was final. While she was speaking a little voice in her head was whispering, 'But you love him, you know you do.' Olivia told Marcia, "I cannot keep repeating the same mistakes and the bastard hurt me so badly. Anyway, after the way I let rip he will be smarting for weeks, and I still don't believe those two girls were Felix's cousins."

Marcia smiled a knowing smile, and she took hold of Wayne's hand as she said, "we are going to see each other now, I have never felt like this before. I know that it seems very quick but will you come back for the wedding?"

Olivia clapped her hands. "Of course, I will, how wonderful." They all laughed and a few hours later they were all fast asleep on the big rugs scattered on the floor.

The following two weeks were extremely busy. Olivia spent her time signing books and contracts. She had planned her work schedule for her next book, which was to be titled 'Bringing on back the good times', and the publishers were still haggling over deadlines. There was too much pressure and Olivia's free spirit was not coping too well. She did not like being dictated to and she wanted to write as and when she wanted. Marcia told her, "It's not a hobby any more, Olivia, it is a job and if you want the money you have to deliver the goods." Olivia knew she had to discipline the rebel within. She knew she had to do it and she would do it!

On her last shopping day Olivia returned to her room to find it full of sunflowers and lilacs. Amidst each bunch of flowers there was a pink rose. In the corner of the room was a pink helium balloon. The message on it said:

Meet at our place on the 21st of October at two p.m. I will wait. I have waited long enough. I love you loads. xxx

Olivia did not want to think about this at all and decided to wait till her flight home when she might have to make some decisions that would affect the rest of her life. She was sick of making decisions and would have been quite happy to drift along in her own little 'Oli' world. She knew that she had to either open a door wider or close it for good. The issue of Adam needed resolving. She unpacked her shopping and began to try the dresses on that she bought that afternoon. She didn't like them all and put some aside for her dear friend Debra who she was always swapping clothes with. This was her last night in New York and she did not want to think. There was always tomorrow. She would think then, not now.

CHAPTER TWENTY-FOUR

It was raining and cold when Olivia left the hotel. She said her goodbyes and left presents for the staff who had looked after her so well. Olivia loved giving presents and seeing people smile. She was ready to go home. Living in the fast lane amongst skyscrapers was not for her. She realised one could not live on the go all the time without burning out and she was so close to breaking down. Not just physically but emotionally. She felt as though she had been through a washing cycle of dirty laundry and she needed to be hung out to dry.

The cabby helped her with her cases and she was soon speeding off to the airport. She wandered around the departure lounge, doing what she did best; shopping! She was not paying much attention to anything as an incredible loneliness swept over her. She watched families and people rushing about and wished for a time to come when she might have at least someone to share her life with.

Through the crowds she saw two people running towards her and a smile changed her face when she saw Marcia and Wayne. They came to a sudden stop in front of her and just avoided knocking her down. Marcia said, "Wow, that was close, we thought we'd missed you." Olivia was so pleased that they had taken the time to come and see her off. Before she could say anything, Marcia thrust the third finger of her left hand out. Sparkling in the airport lights Olivia saw the most beautiful ruby and diamond ring. "We got engaged, and I am taking Wayne up to meet my family on the reservation at the weekend," she said.

Wayne chirped in, "And then I am taking Marcia to London to meet my folks, I hope we might meet up with you? Perhaps come to Yorkshire?"

Olivia congratulated them both and after hugs all round Marcia saw a hat in a shop window and said she would be right back. She had a fetish for hats. Marcia wore a lot of floppy brimmed ones that made her look like a beautiful hippy from the seventies. Wayne took this time alone with Olivia to thank her. "You know I knew there was a reason why we met that day in the park. You are some special lady Olivia and I want you to be in our lives forever."

Olivia looked serious. "Forever is a long time, Wayne. I now hold you dear, you are very like my friend Harry Greenman, and I love you. Are you both sure about all this? You have only known each other two minutes."

Wayne replied, "You know when you know it is the right one, don't you? Haven't you ever just known?" Olivia had 'just known' more times that she cared to remember. She fell in love with love and never waited. Life was too short to wait. One had to grasp at the offerings and deal with the disappointments that followed.

Marcia returned with two bags. "I bought you the same hat Olivia, then we shall always be connected when we wear them." Olivia put her hat on her head and as the flight was called, they all kissed, said their goodbyes and cried. Olivia walked away. It was time to go. She walked out of the departure lounge and out of America. Another chapter in her life closed.

***

Seated at the window watching the clouds go by, sipping a gin and tonic, Olivia smiled at the woman sitting beside her. The woman was rather plump and dressed in an array of colourful swirls that did not quite suit her. She introduced herself with a Midlands accent and said her name was Doreen. Doreen told Olivia she lived in Nottingham and loved Northern Soul music. Olivia said she was a Northern 'Soulie' too. It became apparent to Olivia that Doreen would chat for the whole flight and she was thrown off her guard when Doreen asked, "Haven't I seen you somewhere before?" Olivia expected her to say that she bought her book and recognised her from the picture on the back. What was said next was totally unexpected.

After a few moments of thinking Doreen said, "I have seen you before. You were at the Rolls Royce club with Peers Michaels. It was years ago. You were sat with the Roleys."

Olivia thought, 'Oh my goodness, not again? What is it about planes and the past?'

Olivia gave Doreen a curt reply, "You must be mistaken. I am sorry but I need to get some rest would it be OK if we chatted later?"

Doreen looked embarrassed and apologised. "You are so pretty and she was too. I was sure it was you."

Olivia felt sorry for the dejected Doreen and then said, "Doreen, it was me at the Rolls Royce club but it's hard to talk about."

Doreen patted Olivia's hand. "It's OK dear, it's a long time ago. I didn't mean to upset you."

It wasn't long before Olivia was dreaming of past loves and losses. Characters she knew were fading in and out until one of her memory files opened and she went back to a time when she was at her most vulnerable. She slept for an hour only to be woken by Doreen who was now snoring like a Derbyshire pig beside her. Olivia settled down to read her book. As she opened it a photograph fell out of the back onto her knee. She had this habit of putting photographs in books. She wasn't sure why she did this but felt that it was probably because she had not dealt with the people in the pictures. She was not ready to box off the reminders of other times. She wasn't the only person who boxed events and people in their lives so that when they were able, they could deal with things best forgotten. Olivia turned the picture over to see two smiling faces. She didn't smile. The picture was of her and a man she had met years ago on a dating site. The very same Peers Michaels that Doreen mentioned. Olivia's memories came flooding back uninvited. The universe was at it again!

***

After a marriage of ten years Olivia was restarting her life as a single woman. The world had changed so quickly, and she wasn't going to meet anyone by sitting at her kitchen table. She re-joined the soul scene and after listening to her friend Clare, Olivia joined a dating site. Clare was an avid user of dating sites. She had looked for Mr Right for fifteen years. Olivia should have thought that after fifteen years of looking that perhaps dating sites didn't work.

One Friday evening, Olivia completed a profile and put some pictures up on a page. It wasn't long before the men began to send messages and Olivia was having fun at her kitchen table. Little did she know what was in store for her. After a few one-night stands with unsuitable men, Olivia was contacted by Peers Michaels. He wasn't her usual type.

He had a big nose and black hair. His saving grace was his smile and his big blue eyes. They had a lot in common and soon texts were flowing between them daily. Olivia no longer felt alone. Peers always sent her a text first thing and last thing. It was what she needed at the time and she spent her days glued to the phone. It helped with her loneliness. He made her feel wanted and it wasn't as if she had anything better to do.

They began an online relationship. Olivia learned how to use Skype and soon they were chatting away face to face via the internet. Peers never came online before nine in the evening. Olivia couldn't understand why he always had headphones on and typed his messages. He explained that there was something wrong with the microphone and he would get it fixed. They sent each other photographs of each other and their homes. Peers was into modern soul, and he opened up a whole new genre of music for Olivia, who soon became obsessed with the songs. They even had a song to call theirs. Benny Troy's words were so poignant as he sang, 'I Wanna give you Tomorrow'.

It was the music that bound them. Peers admired Olivia's knowledge of soul music and they were forever playing songs to each other. They became closer and closer until one day Peers asked to meet her. They kept setting dates to meet, but they were always being cancelled by Peers. Olivia was very understanding and said it would happen when it happened. They began to have regular date nights after nine on a Friday. Peers would drink brandy and Olivia would drink wine and more often than not they would get drunk over the airways. Eventually the chat would turn to sex. Olivia wondered if this was called cyber-sex. She had heard about it but never experienced it. Their conversations became lewd until, one night, Olivia showed Peers her breasts and he exposed himself. It was all so silly, they weren't teenagers. It was a natural progression from their banter, and she did not think anything about what she did. Perhaps she should have done. The alcohol flowing through her veins washed away her inhibitions and she did what she did. Things progressed to Olivia talking dirty and Peers playing with himself till he ejaculated. She was not prepared to take her clothes off or anything else after the first time she showed him her magnificent orbs. In fact, she felt that she was mixed up in something she could not now get out of.

One Friday night Olivia drank more than normal and behaved like a drunk lush. She was dancing to the music and Peers was dropping sexual innuendos until she threw caution to the wind and took all her clothes off and continued to dance like an aging hippy without a care in the world.

She forgot where she was as she lost herself in the other worldly sounds of the psychedelia of the late sixties. Transported into a parallel universe, Olivia danced and frolicked and soon forgot to look at the screen. She was partying alone. She did not see Peers playing with himself and having the time of his life at the other end of the Internet. She didn't care. She abandoned herself to the moment as the music became charged with sexual frenzy. This was how it was in the days of LSD. Senses ready to explode as boundaries of the mind were pushed to the limits.

Lysergic acid diethylamide was rather controversial back in the day and famous for its ability to produce hallucinations. Olivia was a young teenager and not quite old enough to enter the world of the sixties fully. She would probably have ended up dead, the drug making her believe that she could fly. It wasn't that long ago that an Australian musician's son fell off a cliff after taking LSD.

LSD may have been good for making music but not that good for prolonging lives. In the sixties and seventies an advocate of the drug was Timothy Leary. He had quite a following and became notorious as he believed that the use of drugs was a good way of exploring the unconscious. Timothy Leary said that "The universe was an intelligence test." What would he have thought of Olivia dancing in front of a computer screen naked and drunk in her living room? He would have thought she was on acid and it wasn't the most intelligent thing Olivia had ever done. As Olivia waited for the next song to begin, she began to come down from her 'high'. She looked at the computer to see a blank screen with no picture. She tapped buttons, she became anxious and sent Peers a text. There was no reply.

Olivia tried to hook up on to Skype again. There was nothing and slowly the curtain began to lift. She knew she'd been had. She had taken her clothes off and danced about like Salome only without the seven veils. What a whore she was! Olivia opened another bottle of wine and took it upstairs where she made a duvet tent, sat under it and rang her friend Clare.

After three hours of crying, drinking wine and admonishing herself on the phone she stopped for breath. Clare took the moment to ask Olivia what she had actually done. Olivia had avoided telling Clare as her friend was rather a prude and would probably not understand. Clare kept asking the question until she said, "I'll tell you what I did then. It's absolutely awful. I can't forgive myself. I just want to die." In between gulps of Merlot and sobs Olivia continued, "I took all my clothes off and danced naked in front of the computer screen."

There was a deafening silence before Clare began to laugh. "Is that all?" They both began to laugh and the cycle of Olivia's despair was broken.

The next day Olivia received a text from Peers explaining that he lost the internet connection and the battery on his phone was flat. He kept trying to reconnect but got fed up and went to bed. Typical of a man to think of himself and not the woman. He hadn't even given her a thought. Olivia never heard the warning bell ringing loudly in the distance. The problem Olivia had was that she didn't listen to anybody and sometimes she also ignored the little voice in her head. She hardly listened to herself either.

Their relationship continued and one day they eventually met in a pub aptly named The Vanish Inn. When they met in the car park there was a chemistry between them, and an observer would have seen the sparks flying. After a few drinks Peers and Olivia were to be found down a country lane with their hands down each other's knickers. They began to meet once a month in a hotel room halfway between their homes. They would have a sex picnic and dance about the room, amongst other things.

Peers couldn't always get an erection but that didn't matter as Olivia would always get her pleasure. Time passed until, one day, Olivia's bubble burst. Clare told her that Peers was married. Clare's friend knew of Peers and he was almost certain that he had a wife. Olivia was not aware of Peers' compulsive lying. When she confronted him, he told the truth! Yes, he was married but they weren't happy. He gave the usual words that married men say when found out and Olivia was taken in by all of his words and the relationship continued.

She believed Peers loved her and that he would leave his wife for her. One day she came home to find Peers sitting on her doorstep with his suitcases. He told her that he had left and was moving in with her. Olivia was at a loss. She had never asked him to leave his wife, even though she hoped he might. She was happy to be the mistress. She was more than happy with their monthly Sunday afternoons. Peers should have asked her first before making such a life changing decision.

Then chaos began. Peers began to bounce about between his wife and Olivia. He left and then he came back. Peers told lies to both women and one day when he was feeling down, he told Olivia he wanted them both. Twice he went back home and then after a few days returned to Olivia's. One fateful Saturday morning the relationship ended forever. The wife rang and gave Peers an ultimatum. She said, "Come home right now or that will be it." Peers had already put their house up for sale. He had the divorce papers ready and had changed his will.

What Olivia did not know was that he had been ringing his wife secretly for days from her greenhouse. So that was to be it. Vera clicked her fingers and the yellow belly decided to cut and run. Olivia had never seen anyone pack so much stuff, so quickly. There were cases and cases.

As Peers made ready to leave, Olivia announced that she wanted all the money she spent on their holidays and solicitors to be repaid. He said he would send her a cheque once he got home. She barred his way and said, "No! You will go into town right now and fetch me the cash." When he left for the bank, she quickly went upstairs and exacted her revenge.

Olivia took her sharpest pair of scissors and cut the buttons off Peers best shirts. She cut a big hole in the back of his favourite sweater and cut the straps of his favourite flip flops. She planted photographs of them both together in strategic places in his bags before spraying her perfume over everything. She took the sex toys they used and put them amongst his shoes and placed pairs of sexy frilly knickers in the pockets of his coats. She could always buy some more. She made sure his bags were as he left them, all locked and ready for the off.

On his return Peers gave her the money he owed and they sat down for a last coffee together. Olivia got on her soap box and began a lecture. "You will regret this. We were happy together and going to have a new life. You are going back to the sad life you came from. You will become bored again and I shall go off and start a new life. Tomorrow I am driving down to Cornwall and don't know if I will come back."

Peers nodded his head and kept saying, "I know, I know." As he got up to leave, he pulled Olivia into his arms and said, "I know I can't come back again, can I?" Olivia began to laugh.

It took a few moments for Olivia to realise that she was not in her kitchen at all but crying on a plane thirty-seven thousand feet above the Atlantic. The woman beside her was still asleep and still snoring like a pig. Olivia ordered a drink and watched the clouds beneath. She looked into the sun. Soon they would be making their descent into Manchester airport and her adventure would be ended. She yearned for the sanctuary of the moors and her cottage. She wondered whether she should write a book about her time in America. It would be a good story. She would have to think about it.

A few hours later Olivia was back in Yorkshire, answering emails and opening post. She decided she would repaint her home before the winter set in and soon, it was mid-October.

CHAPTER TWENTY-FIVE

It was the 21st October and a sunny, warm day; even though the forecast gave out wind and rain. Olivia looked at her watch. There were many reasons why she decided to come up onto the moor so early. Stanley needed a good walk. She idolised her dog and found much pleasure as she watched him running around, sniffing rabbit trails and the scents of other animals that lived in the wild.

Olivia had fully recovered from her trip and America was a distant memory. Now she wanted time to herself. The moor was a good place to think. It was a good place to dream. Most of all she wanted to be here to watch Adam walk towards her. She wanted to watch a speck on the horizon turn into the man she was willing to spend her future with. She had agonised over the decision to meet him and then one morning the voice in her head just said, 'Go for it. He loves you'. It had been a long time coming and she was now admitting to herself that she could never love anyone like she loved Adam. Despite the things he'd done in the past she was prepared to give him a second chance.

Olivia realised that as one got older, one really could not sit about waiting for tomorrow, as tomorrow never comes and one should seize the day. A person creates their own destiny by the acknowledgments and choices they make, and she had made her choice. Soon she would be writing the concluding chapter in an imaginary book called *Searching for True Love*. She had searched for so long. Her whole life was like a film, and she was the heroine. Being objective about herself helped her survive the downs and built up a resilience that kept her positive and focused. Olivia had made many mistakes in her quest to find the love she felt she deserved. Some mistakes were funny, some sad, some interesting, some mad and there were a few total disasters. They all served as character building exercises and the way forward towards what she really wanted.

So, after much thought she made her decision to be here on the moor to meet Adam as he asked when they were in America. Olivia leaned back and felt the cool granite of the Celtic cross on her back. As she looked up at the biggest sky, she remembered all those years ago when she and Adam made love under th cross. She remembered how they chased each other through the heather. She could feel the kisses as though they were only yesterday.

Olivia looked at her watch. There was only another half an hour before she was to move on to the next phase of her life. She felt the excitement building up in her stomach. The butterflies were there as they woke up and did somersaults of happiness deep inside her gut. She would cry no more as she looked forward to the love she needed. Olivia now knew that she had needed time to grow up and calm down. She had certainly done that, but it didn't seem so now, as she became giddy with anticipation.

She kept chuckling and spoke to herself, as one does when they can't really believe something. She couldn't remember when she last felt so happy. Her eyes sparkled and her skin was glowing, a soft sheen of tan covered her face. Olivia still looked younger than her years and she smiled as she thought about her trip to America. She had dealt with the muddy waters of her past and now there was clarity in her future. Her decision finally made.

Even though she loved travelling and new experiences with lots of activity, Olivia never stopped yearning for home and the moor. Now she was here with her best friend by her side. Stanley was so tuned in to Olivia. They travelled life's highway together and he was her number one buddy. She took in the panorama of the moor. The gentle breeze was blowing the cotton flowers and the heather was turning the landscape into a beautiful purple lavender hue.

Olivia looked at her watch again. Time was moving too slow for her just now. She rose and walked away from the cross, calling Stanley to follow her. He gave her such joy as he bounced about like a spring lamb in the bracken. She walked towards the gate that she knew Adam would come through. She lay down in a mossy dip. Stanley ran to her and lay down beside her. They were inseparable. Stanley had never let her down. He had never lied to her, and he had never used and abused her. His unconditional love was amazing. Why couldn't men be more like dogs?

Olivia was a sky watcher. It was a therapeutic way of relieving stress. She was feeling a little stressed as she waited for the clock to strike the hour. Today the sky was filled with cotton wool clouds that made shapes and images that motivated the imagination. Was that a heart floating by? Was that a duck? The clouds rolled across the sky like the surf on the ocean and now America and her past were oceans away as her mind sailed across on the moor.

As Olivia ran her fingers through the short grass, she began to talk to herself, the words quietly roaming about in her mind 'I am so lucky to be here, and my patience has paid off. The love I thought I had all those years ago, I know I now have. I can't believe I carried it locked away for so long. I know what I want, and I am prepared to walk off into the sunset with my dreams and into the dawn of the rest of my life. How lucky am I? After all the idiots I have kissed and now to come full circle back to where I started, and my chaos began. What I was searching for was always there stored in the archives of my memories. Things don't happen when you want them. They happen when the universe wants them to happen. We were all on that plane to America for a reason. Now I know what that reason was.'

Olivia's mind went back to that fateful day when she was walking down the aisle of the plane that was taking her to New York. No coincidence then that Adam and Felix were sitting together? No coincidence that the three of them were on the same plane together in the sky over the Atlantic? They were the good, the bad and the ugly. Olivia was the good. Felix was the ugly, for the terrible way he treated her without explanation. Apologising twenty years later did not put right what he did. Adam was the bad, for what he did to her but now he was the good and he was her future.

A bird flew overhead, and Olivia watched it gliding on the airwaves. She was reminded of her favourite book, *Jonathan Livingstone Seagull* by Richard Bach. The story touched Olivia's soul and she found it easy to identify with the bird that wouldn't fly with the pack. Soon she would fly away with her Adam. She had waited so long for this and now the time was nearly here.

There were ten more minutes to go, and Olivia decided to walk back to the cross. She ran the last few yards. As she turned to see if Stanley was with her, she saw a dot on the horizon and her heart missed a beat. It leapt high in her chest and began to dance to the rhythm of her breathing. He was coming. She began to shake and beads of sweat appeared on her forehead. Olivia peered into the distance as the dot became larger. The person came nearer, and Olivia saw that they had a limp. A large brown dog bounded up to Stanley and they began to play chase. Disappointment put the ocean that was swirling round in Olivia's gut to sleep, as she saw it was not Adam.

As panic set in Olivia searched for her phone. She was distracted by a quad bike coming down the track. It passed by her. She could not find her phone. She must have left it on the kitchen table. It might not have been any good as the signal came and went so high up on the moor. Ringing Adam to see where he was might suggest that she did not trust him and that would just not do. A woman needed to keep her dignity, watch her demeanour and never appear over eager. Olivia learnt this the hard way. Her enthusiasm lost her many a man, as she once wandered the lonely lanes of 'you can get instant love here for a price.'

She sat down by the cross, and ever the romantic drama queen she imagined the scene when she would look up into the dark brown eyes of the man standing above her. Their eyes would meet, and he would hold out his hand to her, pull her up towards him as his lips opened up to meet hers in a long 'Hello'. The passion would flow through their veins, merging at the places where their bodies were touching. She would be Catherine to his Heathcliff, up on the moor under the sun. One thing Olivia was never short of was imagination. The storyteller in her never really slept.

As her mind wandered, it began to drift, and Olivia was soon asleep. She was happily sailing through her dreams. Bobbing about on the waves of her imagination. She could see a yacht on the horizon, a man standing on the bow looking towards her. It would land before her. She flew to a beach where she stood naked with Adam. Anything can happen in dreams. She lay with him in the dunes and felt his mouth gently suck on her nipple as his hand slowly caressed her free breast. She moaned in her sleep. The soft scent of lavender wafted across the shore and the ocean sang to her.

Don't wake me up if I should be dreaming.
I don't want to miss one minute of this dream.
Oceans away, go where you may.
Love will be with you, oceans away.

In dreams anything can happen, and a butterfly landed on Olivia's hand. She did not move. "Do you have a name?"

The butterfly replied, "I have. My name is 'love'."

Another butterfly landed next to Love and said, "My name is 'Elusive'." Olivia tried to catch hold of the butterflies and they flew away.

One butterfly came back and said, "You cannot hold me. If you catch me, you will eventually have to let go. I shall come and go as I please. You may crave for me and want me, but I do not fly to your orders. You have no power over me, but I have power over you. You cannot own me. I am not a commodity. I will be yours or I won't. It's my choice. Some people search for me and never find me. My name is the 'elusive butterfly of love'." The butterfly flew away. In her dream, Olivia sat up and looked at the ocean. She sat watching the sun go down until the stars came out and she was surrounded by darkness.

She woke with a start as Stanley rolled his wet pink tongue over her face. She jumped up, startled, and for some reason looked round expecting to see a butterfly until she realised that she had been dreaming. She was disorientated and noticed that the sun was on its way down. She looked at her watch. It was way past two o' clock and Adam was now late. She became anxious as she remembered her dream. Could it have been an omen? Was he not coming? He had let her down in the past. He hurt her so badly. He could do it again. She began to generalise about men. Too many had let her down in her quest to find love. They only thought of themselves, their shallowness determined by the size of the brain between their legs. Men like that created mayhem and left devastation behind them.

Olivia knew there were good men out there, somewhere. She had yet to find one. She pulled herself up and spoke sharply to herself. "Of course, he will come. He probably got held up somewhere." She waited till six. During that time, she relived her time at Cape May and remembered all the things Adam said to her. She remembered Raines Law Room with embarrassment where she said things in anger and yet he still asked her to meet him on this day. Yes, not to worry, Adam would come.

Adam did not come.

CHAPTER TWENTY-SIX

Raindrops began to fall as the sun disappeared behind a large sheet of grey and a chilling wind began to blow, Olivia ran back to her car. With each raindrop a tear began to run down her face. She gasped as anguish engulfed her. With each step her pain of disappointment sharpened and when she reached the safe haven of her car, the floodgates opened. She was cold and miserable. She sobbed, she heaved, she gasped for breath as her anxiety gave way to a mammoth feeling of despair. It was a long time since Olivia had had an anxiety attack. She was having one now. Anxiety attacks can be caused by many things and usually peak in about ten minutes. Olivia cried for herself, she cried for all the promises that were broken down the years. She cried for her lost trust and the disappointment that it always brought. She cried for her naivety which always made her so vulnerable. It wasn't as though she was ugly or a bad person. She wasn't stupid but perhaps not very intelligent where men were concerned. Why did this always happen? Why could she not catch the butterfly? Why was it so elusive?

Her rationality stepped in to help and she jumped out of the car and gave out a large, long scream. Poor Stanley thought she had gone mad. She knew what she was doing, and the tension soon left her body, and she opened her arms to the elements and allowed the rain to wash away her angst.

She sat for a while looking across the rain-sodden moor. When the sun went down it was the worst place in the world to be. It was wild and relentless in its harshness. Olivia really did not want to go home. She had nothing to go home for. She thought Adam might have saved her from the loneliness of old age. She put all her hopes into Adam and his words. She had believed him when he said he wanted to try again. He had now let her down once more and she was feeling very foolish. She turned the ignition and, with a large sigh, drove away. Olivia really had to get a grip. Her mind was shrouded in a mist of confusion as she left her hopes and dreams amongst the bracken on the moor.

As Olivia put the key in her lock, she heard the phone ringing. She saw the light flashing as she peered through the frosted glass. She began to fumble and too soon the ringing stopped. 'Never mind,' she thought. It was probably Anne wanting to know how things went with Adam. Anne had grave doubts about Olivia and Adam getting back together and she still could not call him by name. He would remain 'that bastard!' forever.

Olivia poured herself a large glass of comfort. The red liquid of the Pinot Noir warmed her, and she sat in the window seat watching the day turn into night. The knife of disappointment began to twist in her gut, and she began to cry. What was there worth living for? Why did she go on? There were many times in her life Olivia thought about what she called, 'Going home'. She would never kill herself but at her lowest moments wished she could walk off the planet and go home to a place where things were different and much better.

When she was all cried out, Olivia looked at herself in the window. Her reflection spoke to her vanity, and she was soon showering in the bathroom. A cold spurt at the end cleared her aura and she was ready to pick up the pieces of her broken ego and her broken heart. It was time to make a plan. She decided to ring Anne. Anne would make her laugh and they would arrange to have a girly day out. She returned to the kitchen and put the kettle on. Sitting down at the large table she turned her phone over. Olivia saw there were six missed calls, and the light was flashing to show she had a voice mail. She knew it would be her chirpy friend asking where she was. Olivia rang Anne. "Hiya, sorry I didn't get your calls Anne. I left my phone at home. Did you want me for anything?" Anne sounded puzzled, "no I didn't, I was just wondering if you are, ok?" "Yes, I am fine." Olivia replied, "I'm going to have an early night, love you and see you tomorrow." Just before Anne put the phone down, she said, "by the way, it wasn't me who rang you I have been out all day."

Olivia looked at the red light that was still flashing and pressed the button to retrieve the message, she thought was from Anne. The loudspeaker became a portal for words as she went to make a cup of tea. Olivia nearly spilled the hot water from the kettle onto her hand as she heard Adam's voice. "Olivia I am so sorry. Please pick up the phone. I won't be there at two as we agreed. I have an urgent meeting. Why aren't you answering your phone? When you get this message, please ring me back." Olivia was stunned and pressed the button again to retrieve the next message.

She heard Adam's voice again. "I could come round to yours, but it might be late. I need to explain about Felix and his cousins. Please Olivia, pick up the phone, answer me. I won't set off until I hear from you." There was a moment's pause and she heard Adam cough, before he carried on. "Olivia, I love you. I have always loved you. I will make everything up to you. We shall be together. Call me when you get this message, please?"

Olivia noticed that the messages were recorded before the time they should have met. If she had not left early, she would have received them. Why had she forgotten her phone? She never forgot her phone. Olivia's heart began to beat faster and pounded in her chest. She stared at the phone, looked out of the window and down at the floor. A butterfly stirred in her stomach. It was the one from her dream. The one called 'love'. She forgot about the tea and took a bottle of Pinot Noir out of the cupboard. She needed to feel the sweet red liquid. She needed solace. She struggled with the top and found herself getting stressed as she was unable to pull the cork. A tear left her eye as she gave one last pull and there was a pop. She went back to her phone and saw that another voicemail had come through when she was in the shower.

There was silence at the beginning of the message and then Olivia heard Adam's voice again. This time he sounded flat, the zest gone from his voice as he said very slowly, "I don't know why you aren't answering. I guess you changed your mind. I knew it was too good to be true, you giving me another chance. My bad! I could not believe my luck when I saw you on the plane and then in Cape May. I wanted you so much. I wanted to spend the rest of my life with you. I wanted to make it up to you. Perhaps it wasn't what you wanted. I can understand why you won't talk to me. Well, my sweet Olivia, I wish you all the best. I hope you find the happiness you deserve. I mean that. You and I were obviously not meant to be. Have a nice life, love. I won't be calling again. I am gone."

Olivia sat very still. She was stunned by Adam's words. How could he blow hot and cold over a couple of hours? Olivia turned the phone over in her hand. "What shall I do now?" She asked herself if perhaps she should ring him back. Perhaps that would not be a good idea, his message made it quite clear that it was over before it had begun. His voice sounded as harsh as it did all those years ago when he destroyed her.

She went and sat out on the patio. The rain stopped as she watched the twinkling lights of the houses across the valley. The stars were coming out above her and she began to cry again. Slowly the outer layer of her heart started to peel. With each teardrop that fell, another layer fell from the onion of her love. Strangled by emotion Olivia felt the shadow of despair run across her soul.

A large sigh left her, and she sat quietly, not thinking. It was quite dark now. She could not believe her eyes as a butterfly landed on the plant next to her. She wondered where it came from. Olivia sat very still, and put out her hand. The butterfly flew onto her palm, and they sat looking at each other for a while. She turned away to look at the kitchen clock through the window and when she turned back her palm was empty.

Olivia felt a strange disappointment and an unwelcome anger began to rise inside. She got up and threw her glass out into the drive where it smashed into a thousand pieces. She ran into the kitchen and took a notebook and pen out of the drawer. It was times like this that she could access the core of her passion. She needed to write. In a frenzy, she covered the page in a mass of words which she read back to herself.

I have escaped to my dreams now that you have taken my reality.

I only have each minute, as you have stolen my tomorrow.

I see a beach and the ocean through the fog of my despair.

A figure of sadness dances alone. Is it you or I?

I dance alone without you. I keep you but you are oceans away.

You walk alone without me, not feeling my hand in yours.

You left me in my dream that was once a reality.

Tomorrow is as invisible as the moon on a sunny day.

Shrouded in my hopelessness and the emptiness of love, you took my smile as I drown in the ocean of life.

I wait foolishly for you to exchange it for the tears you left behind.

Until then my lost love, I shall wander on the beach of promises.

I shall look for you over the ocean of my dreams.

I shall dance alone with my sadness.

Olivia sat with her silence until her phone came alive. Ruby Andrews' beautiful voice began to sing, 'Just loving you'. She knew it would be Anne again, who had probably forgotten to tell her something, and she really did not want to speak to anyone right now. She had some decisions to make.

The ringing stopped and after a few moments began again. With a big sigh Olivia pressed the answer button. "Hello, this is Olivia," she whispered.

The reply came, "Hello, this is Adam."

To be continued…

PLAYLIST

Nobody	Keith Sweat
Albinoni	Adagio in G minor
I will always love you	Hauser/Senorita
Soldier Blue	Buffy St Marie
Closure	Gabrielle
Walk in my shoes	Gladys Knight
I walked away	Bobby Paris
Dandelion	Rolling Stones
Paper back writer/Ticket to Ride/And I love him/Eleanor Rigby/She's leaving home	The Beatles
Love of the loved	Cilla Black
And I love him	Esther Phillips
Let's get married	Al Green
I am a man of constant sorrow	Soggy Bottom Boys
The best is yet to come	Sandy Barber
Oceans away	Phillip Goodhand Tait
How deep is your love	Bee Gees
This too shall pass	India Arie
Tango in the night	Fleetwood Mac
A taste of Honey	Four tops and the Supremes
Just loving you	Ruby Andrews
You do something to me	Dorothy Dandridge
Don't bring Lulu	Dorothy Provine
If I ain't go you	Alicia Keys
Home is where the heart is	Bobby Womack
Don't send nobody else	Ace Spectrum
I wanna give you tomorrow	Benny Troy